"Why was there a tea~~m~~ my father's deat~~h?~~

So she'd put two and two together already, had she? She obviously hadn't missed anything, though he wished he could go back in time and replay his first phone call to her. If he'd had it to do over again, he'd have told her from the beginning that there was some possibility her father had been murdered.

Because if anything, it was worse having to tell her now.

"We suspected he may have been murdered." He watched her carefully as she absorbed the news. No screams, no crying, not even a gasp.

"And the fact that somebody broke into the house?"

"It's hard to say at this point," Gideon tempered his response, "but there's a very good chance the two are related."

...cCalla

...ve Inspired Suspense

...a Instinct
...oubled Waters
Out on a Limb
Danger on Her Doorstep

RACHELLE MCCALLA

is a mild-mannered housewife, and the toughest she ever has to get is when she's trying to keep her four kids quiet in church. Though she often gets in over her head, as her characters do, and has to find a way out, her adventures have more to do with sorting out the carpool and providing food for the potluck. She's never been arrested, gotten in a fistfight or been shot at. And she'd like to keep it that way! For recipes, fun background notes on the places and characters in this book and more information on forthcoming titles, visit www.rachellemccalla.com.

DANGER ON HER DOORSTEP

RACHELLE McCALLA

Steeple
Hill®

Published by Steeple Hill Books™

STEEPLE HILL BOOKS

Steeple
Hill®

Recycling programs
for this product may
not exist in your area.

ISBN-13: 978-0-373-44427-4

DANGER ON HER DOORSTEP

Copyright © 2011 by Rachelle McCalla

www.SteepleHill.com

Printed in U.S.A.

Unless the Lord builds the house,
its builders labor in vain.
—*Psalm* 127:1

To Henry, Eleanor, Genevieve and Knox.
You inspire me every day.

Acknowledgments

A super big thank-you to my amazing editor Emily Rodmell, without whose keen insights and editorial prowess this book wouldn't be nearly so good, if it even existed at all.

Never-ending thanks to my husband, Ray McCalla, for picking up the kids and folding the laundry and all the other bazillion ways you take up the slack so I can write. I love you.

Tremendous thanks to Deputy Charles McCalla of the Page County Sheriff's Department, and my father, retired Police Sergeant Brian Richter, for all your keen answers to even my most bizarre questions. You make me look like I know what I'm talking about.

Huge, huge, huge thanks to all the booksellers and newspaper editors and the wonderful staff at KTCH radio who've helped to spread the word about my books.

Terrific thanks to my readers. You honor me by choosing to read my stories.

And most of all, eternal thanks to my Lord and Savior Jesus Christ, who paid it all already. You make everything possible.

ONE

Maggie Arnold felt uneasy about being alone in the old house on Shady Oak Lane, and it wasn't just because her father died here. The rambling old building was full of sheet-draped furniture which hunkered in the shadows.

But it was now or never. She had to push her fears aside and get the project started if she ever wanted to leave this house behind her. She pulled out her phone.

In her haste, Maggie had the call ringing through before she realized she hadn't asked for the name of the handyman whose number her Realtor had given her.

A deep voice answered her call. "Hello?" He sounded strong. Capable. Could she tell that much from one word?

"I'm calling for the handyman," Maggie started, embarrassed that she didn't know his name. "Susan Isakson gave me this number."

"I'll be sure to thank her for the referral. What's the project?" So he was cordial, too.

Maggie's heart gave a little flip, which she told herself was silly. There was no reason for her to get too excited at the sound of a strong man's voice. She just hoped this guy would be able to help her with the house she'd inherited when her father had died a little over two weeks ago.

Otherwise she didn't know where else to turn. "Do you know the old Victorian on Shady Oak Lane?"

The man let out an almost silent groan.

Maggie couldn't stand the idea that she'd lose him so easily. She rushed on. "I know it's a big project, but I'm willing to do a lot of the work myself. If you'd at least come take a look at it, even if you could just do part of it—"

"I can stop by this afternoon."

"You can?" Maggie nearly screeched in her relief. None of the other contractors she'd called had even offered to take a look at the house, and she had to have help—soon.

"Say around four o'clock?"

That was in less than a half hour. "That would be perfect."

"And, let's see…" the deep voice paused "…you're Maggie Arnold, right?"

"Right."

"Okay, see you at four, then."

"See you then." Maggie hung up the phone with a breathless goodbye and leaned her elbows back on the staircase where she sat, looking up the wide-open stairwell at the dizzying pattern of exposed stud walls above her, wondering how the handyman knew her name when she didn't even know his.

Oh, he'd probably heard all about her already. After living in Kansas City since she'd graduated from high school, Maggie wasn't used to Holyoake, Iowa, anymore, where the scant five thousand townspeople knew everything about everybody and who was up to what. No doubt rumors were already flying about her return to town and what would become of the house on Shady Oak Lane.

Most people probably figured she wasn't up to the task of fixing it up. She figured they were probably right.

And this handyman guy—whatever his name was—from his reaction, she could assume he already knew how much trouble the house would be. It was entirely possible he was only stopping by to be nice, and had no real intention of taking on the project. But she *had* to have his help. Though she'd meant it when she'd said she could help with the work, she didn't know much about construction—just enough to know she wasn't up to tackling the project alone.

And she'd already been turned down by every other contractor in town. Their excuses echoed through her mind. *Too busy. No longer in business. Only new construction. No major renovations.* And perhaps the most ominous of all: *I wouldn't go near that house for anything.*

"Neither would I," Maggie whispered to herself, "if it were only up to me." But she didn't have much choice in the matter. The house needed so much work. She looked around her at the aging plaster and woodwork coated with decades of paint. Her eyes fell on a couple of dead bats in the corner of the foyer. At least, she hoped they were dead.

Closing her eyes to the sight, she pictured instead the faces of children who'd been patients in the pediatric ward at the hospital where she worked in Kansas City. The new children's wing addition would be such a blessing to so many. Once she got the house fixed up enough to sell, she could make a large donation to the project and have one of the rooms named after her father. She'd already listed the other rental houses she'd inherited, but her dad had gutted most of the second floor of the old Victorian, and the Realtor had assured her the only way she'd get any profit from the house would be if she returned it to habitable condition first.

"Dear Lord," Maggie prayed, closing her eyes tight against the sight of the overwhelming amount of work that needed to be done, "help me. *Please* soften this man's heart so he'll be willing to take on this project." She felt a stab of fear as she wondered why this nameless handyman was able to stop by on such short notice. Why wasn't he busy at four in the afternoon? "And please let him be a good man. I don't need any more problems."

Former Sheriff Gideon Bromley slid the phone back into his pocket and made a face, stomping his foot to let out some of the frustration he felt. Why? Why had he just agreed to take a look at Maggie Arnold's project? He knew better, didn't he? But the lawman inside him just couldn't let a case go unsolved—even if he no longer had his badge.

Ever since that morning two weeks before when he'd found Glen Arnold lying facedown on the cellar floor of that old Victorian house, things in his own life had quickly careened out of control. Labor Day weekend had been a busy one. While he'd been busy on the job trying to sort out what had happened at the house on Shady Oak Lane, his own brother had been using him to gain access to information on a meth production investigation that had broken wide-open.

Worst of all, his brother, Bruce, had been the person producing the drugs. While Gideon was distracted investigating Glen Arnold's death, Bruce had covered his tracks by framing innocent people for his own illegal activities. And when the DEA swept in, Bruce had tried to pass the guilt onto Gideon.

Gideon had stepped down from his job as sheriff

pending a full inquiry into his involvement with his brother's crimes. At this point, he didn't even know what the status was on Glen Arnold's murder investigation. If he was smart, he'd stay away from anything having to do with the case or the crime scene, including staying as far as possible from the house on Shady Oak Lane.

But Maggie Arnold sounded desperate, and his heart went out to her. Besides, he didn't know what else to do with his time while he waited for the verdict to be handed down. He'd come up with the idea of doing handyman work the week before. Even after hanging up posters and running an ad in the local paper, he hadn't found a single person who wanted the suspended sheriff working on their house.

Though their rejection stung, Gideon understood. They felt betrayed at the thought that the official they'd elected had been running illegal drugs right under their noses. Except that he *hadn't* been running drugs. That was just Bruce's story.

But of course, everyone believed Bruce. Gideon's much older brother had long been one of the most respected men in town, mostly because he owned a transportation company that was one of the biggest employers in the county. Ironically, it seemed the transportation company had been just one more cog in the wheel in Bruce's meth production and distribution ring. And much of Bruce's well-respected wealth had come from drug money. Though Bruce was now behind bars, his influence remained.

Worst of all, Bruce had used his little brother's position as sheriff as an inside means of gathering information so he could stay one step ahead of any investigation that might have uncovered his illegal activities. While Gideon had been at the house on Shady Oak Lane, Bruce had been at the sheriff's station, supposedly waiting to see him, but actually monitoring the progress of the drug investigation.

The old Victorian on Shady Oak Lane had been the wrong place for him to be that weekend. Unfortunately, there was no way he could go back in time and do things differently. All he could do was press on.

As he pulled on his work boots and made sure he had whatever tools he might need, Gideon decided it didn't matter, really, what had happened at that old house, or how his life had been changed by it. Work was work. And he needed something to fill his time before he drove himself crazy with all his regrets.

At the sound of knocking Maggie looked up from the long list she'd been making of things the house needed done. Through the beveled glass door inset she could clearly see a man's broad-shouldered silhouette. He was early. Was that a good sign?

She didn't know, but scrambled to open the door for him. Giving the age-warped door a couple of hard tugs, she finally popped it open, and extended her hand toward the figure on the other side.

Long fingers closed around her proffered hand. "Hi. You called for a handyman?"

The strong voice sounded the same as it had over the phone, but Maggie couldn't see anything of the man's face against the backdrop of bright sunlight as the autumn afternoon sun blazed low in the sky behind him. She fought the urge to immediately pull back from him. It was a simple handshake. Maggie had shaken hands with hundreds of people since she'd been back, between her father's funeral and all the meetings dealing with his estate. So why did this handshake feel so different? His touch sent her heartbeat racing.

Telling herself she was just nervous about his assessment of the overwhelming remodeling project, she pulled her hand away and practically leaped back into the foyer to make room for him to step inside. "Thanks for stopping by. Come on in. Have you ever been in this house before?"

"Uh, yes," the deep voice rumbled. "Yes, actually. Just a couple of weeks ago."

As she closed the door behind him, Maggie blinked back the glaring red that had imprinted on her retinas. She looked up at the man who seemed to fill the large foyer, wishing her vision would clear so she could see his face. Her heart was still hammering inside her, and the way his wide shoulders loomed over her didn't help. Though part of his height could be attributed to his thick-heeled work boots, the man was still close to six feet tall—much taller than her squat five foot two. And kind of scary since they were alone on the outskirts of town, in the house where her father had died.

Chastising herself for letting her fear get the better of her, she startled as the face above her came into focus. The square chin had a deep cleft in the middle that was mirrored by the ridge between his arched black brows. He had a fierce, hard face. Dark eyes glinted down at her as Maggie recognized the man. A jolt of panic sped through her.

No! She wished she could push him back out of her house, but the door was already closed behind her. Did he still hate her after all these years? Did he still blame her father for what had happened two decades before?

"Gideon." The name dropped from her lips in a lifeless whisper. What was he doing here, anyway? "I thought you were the sheriff." Her eyes narrowed as her fear-frozen brain started working again. But no, she'd heard people talking…

"I was. Two weeks ago when I called you with the news about your father, I was the sheriff. I've stepped down pending an investigation into my involvement in a meth production ring that was operating out of Holyoake County."

That was what she'd heard about him. Everyone had been talking about it at the funeral. "Did you do it?" The question escaped before her stunned consciousness could hold it back.

While she watched, Gideon's full lips bent upward in an amused expression, chasing the hardness from his face until he smiled right up to his eyes. A chuckle burst from him, surprising her. "You know, I think you're the first person who's ever actually asked me that. Everyone else just assumed I'm guilty."

Maggie tittered nervously along. The man didn't look quite so intimidating when he smiled, though she could see how he'd make a great lawman. Probably scared the daylights out of the bad guys.

Gideon's laughter faded quickly, and he explained, "Actually, I didn't do any of the things they're accusing me of. I knew there were drugs coming out of this county, but I had no idea my brother was the person behind their production. And to my shame, I was oblivious that he was using *me* to get the information he needed to make sure his operation went undetected." The smile disappeared, replaced by a much more frightening jaded expression. "Not that my innocence will make one bit of difference against the evidence he's stacked up against me."

"So, you don't think you'll get your job back?" Maggie tried to keep the uneasy shiver out of her voice. She almost succeeded.

"Doubt it. I'll probably go to prison instead." He stepped back and looked around him, obviously done discussing the subject. "Where do you want to start?"

Maggie followed his lead and looked around, feeling lost in the midst of the multitude of projects the house would need to have finished before it could be sold. New plumbing, new walls, new...everything. She gulped.

Gideon spun back around from his survey of the foyer and faced her. "Unless you don't want an accused man working on your house. You can tell me to get lost. I'd understand."

He'd somehow ended up closer to her, and Maggie could see the pain behind his brown-black eyes. Up until she'd recognized him, she'd been praying with all her might the handyman would be willing to work on the house. Now she wasn't sure what she wanted. "You're not just offering that because you don't want the headache of taking on this project, are you?" she asked him directly. "I wouldn't blame you if you didn't want to have anything to do with this place."

His dark eyes glinted as he looked down at her, obviously trying to size up whether she was being straightforward with him or playing some kind of game. Yup, the bad guys would be shaking in their boots right now.

Maggie didn't feel too brave, either, but she'd faced a lot of frightening situations in her job as a nurse in the pediatric ward. Gideon Bromley didn't scare her—too much.

Gideon's stony face softened slightly. "Do you realize I'm the man who found your father's body?"

The backward step she took toward the door was completely involuntary. "*You* did?" Her confidence in his innocence wavered slightly. What if this man really had done all those illegal things people accused him of? But she'd known Gideon Bromley since junior high school.

He'd been intimidating even then.

"Yes. How much have you been told about what happened?"

"I—I—" Maggie faltered, looking around, trying to think. What had Gideon been doing at the house on Shady Oak Lane that Saturday morning? "They haven't told me anything, really, just that he had a broken neck. I wasn't looking for details."

That seemed to censor him. "Sorry to bring it up. I just didn't want there to be any awkwardness if I'm going to be working here with you."

Maggie told herself to resume breathing. "It's okay. Obviously reminders of him are everywhere." As if to make her point, her eyes traveled toward the back of the house, where the door to the cellar where her father's body had been found was located just out of sight.

Gideon turned to glance in the direction where she was looking. "Have you been to the basement?"

"Only once."

"Would you like to start there?"

Maggie felt her heart give a little squeeze. Did she want to revisit the place where her father had died? No. She wanted her father back alive, but that wasn't an option. She looked up at Gideon and was surprised by the less-than-fierce expression on his face. Was that kindness behind his eyes?

She took a gulp, stepped toward the back of the house and tried to interject a casual tone into her voice. "Sounds like as good a place as any." Judging by the way the words faded before she finished her sentence, she knew her attempt at nonchalance had failed.

Maggie led Gideon through the cavernous rooms to

the narrow back stairwell that descended to the basement. They stepped down into the musty dark. Two sets of stairs led into the subterranean space. The narrow stairs they'd used came down from inside the house near the kitchen. The other set came in from outside the house in the back-yard. A sliver of light marked the opening to the wide cellar doors that led outside—the stairs where her father had died.

With a pull on the chain of the lone lightbulb that dangled from the low ceiling, sickly yellow light filled the room. Unable to look at the door or the floor, Maggie turned her attention to Gideon.

He seemed furious. "They didn't even clean up?"

Maggie glanced down at the broken pieces of porce-lain tiles that littered the floor. She understood her father had been carrying a box of tiles when he'd fallen, which had split open and shattered upon impact with the floor. "Who?"

"The investigation team. They should have at least swept up the pieces of tiles once they were done with the site. That's just common courtesy."

"What investigation team?"

"From the sheriff's office." Gideon bent down and started scooping broken tiles into a pile.

Maggie bent to help him in slow motion, her mind stuck on what he'd said. "Why did they need an investigation team?"

"To determine whether his death was an accident or—" Gideon's hands swept close to hers, and he looked up at her. His mouth clamped shut.

"Or what?" Maggie looked at him quizzically. She'd never heard that there was ever any question about how her father had died. "Gideon?"

He looked down at the pile of tile pieces between them,

the shiny fragments a stark contrast to the dull cement floor. Slowly, he let the last few chips in his hands drop into the pile with tiny clinking sounds. "Was your father's death ruled accidental?"

"Of course."

"Then pretend I didn't say anything." He rose and dusted his hands off on his dark jeans. "Is there a broom upstairs?"

Maggie didn't feel at all comfortable about his sudden change of subject, but she went ahead and answered his question. "Not that I know of, but I saw one in the garage earlier." She stood, dusting her hands off, as well. "Here, you can go out through the cellar door."

They both moved toward the wooden double doors that closed off the outside cellar stairs from the inside. Maggie froze as she reached for the drop bar that secured the door. "Wait a second."

The door hung loosely on its hinges. The two-by-four that had been used to bar entry had been pushed in. Bolts protruded between the wooden door frame and the brick-and-mortar foundation, as though the door had been forced open from the outside.

"Was the door like that before?" Gideon asked from behind her.

"No." Maggie didn't have to think about her answer. She'd stood in that exact spot the day before and leaned on the drop bar while she wept for her father. Though her eyes had been blurry with tears, she had no doubt the door she'd seen and leaned on then had been securely attached it its frame. Now it was pulled ajar, dangling loosely, as if someone had rammed it open in order to gain entry.

Gideon stepped past her and gave the frame a gentle tug. It gaped inward a good foot or more—plenty wide enough to allow a person to enter through the space. "Let's get upstairs," he whispered suddenly.

"Do you think someone broke in?" Maggie asked.

"Looks like it." Gideon's hand fell to her arm, encouraging her back toward the narrow staircase that led to the kitchen in the back of the house. "And for all we know, they could still be in here."

TWO

Gideon didn't want to frighten Maggie, but he needed first and foremost to ensure her safety. Obviously the basement wasn't secure, not with the door hanging from its frame. And for that matter, neither was the rest of the house. If someone had broken in, they could be hiding anywhere in the sprawling dwelling. Gideon had his own theories on how Maggie's father had died. If he was right, there was a killer on the loose.

"Why don't we head outside?" he asked as they stepped into the sunlit kitchen.

"We can go out the back door and see what the cellar doors look like from out there," Maggie said with only a faint tremor running through her words.

Gideon's heart clenched. Poor thing. She was holding together pretty well, considering. "Excellent idea," he encouraged her as they stepped out onto the aged brick patio and turned toward where the triangular cellar doors let out from the basement. He groaned as they approached.

The hinges had been pulled free of the aging wood. The break-in job probably hadn't been very difficult—a crowbar would do it. But what disturbed him even more was the fact that whoever had made entry into the house hadn't even tried to hide what they'd done.

Why weren't they more careful? Why weren't they afraid?

"Gideon?" Maggie's voice came out too highpitched.

He turned his attention back to her and realized the situation was catching up with her. This couldn't be easy for her to see. "Let's have a seat a second," he suggested, taking her by the arm and guiding her toward an old double glider by the garage. The rusty old swing had obviously spent too many winters outside, but it looked sturdy enough to hold them.

Gideon sat down beside her.

"What was it?" she asked, the fear in her blue eyes magnified by the curvature of her thick-rimmed glasses. "Why was there a team investigating my father's death? Do you think someone may have killed him?"

So she'd put two and two together already, had she? Gideon recalled from their school days that she was pretty bright. She obviously hadn't missed anything this time, either, though he wished he could go back in time and replay his first phone call to her. If he'd had to do it over again, he'd have told her from the beginning that there was some possibility her father had been murdered.

Because if anything, it was worse having to tell her now.

"We suspected he may have been murdered." He watched her carefully as she absorbed the news. No screams, no crying, not even a gasp. She just kept staring at the broken cellar door.

After a minute, she took a gulp and asked, "And the fact that somebody broke into the house?"

"It's hard to say at this point," Gideon said, tempering

his response, "but there's a very good chance the two are related."

She nodded slowly. "Why would the murderer return?"

"I don't know." Gideon didn't want her getting any more worked up than she already was. Besides, they needed to call the sheriff's office. If it had been his house, he'd have placed the call already. But then, his house, though only a couple of blocks from this one, was inside the city limits, and the Holyoake cops would have answered the call. The house on Shady Oak Lane was outside of town, and therefore in the sheriff's territory.

Since he wasn't supposed to have anything to do with the ongoing sheriff's investigations, he needed to leave well enough alone. The last thing he wanted to do was make it look as though he was trying to heavy-hand a case. If he ever wanted to be sheriff again, he needed to respect the boundaries that had been erected. Which meant Maggie would need to place the call.

"Do you have your phone on you? Can you call the sheriff's office to come investigate?"

She looked up at him with wide eyes. Funny, he'd always thought her plain before. Mousy brown hair, dorky glasses, a little on the short side. But close-up, her thick, long eyelashes fluttered against her lightly freckled cheekbones. Maggie Arnold was pretty.

Gideon shook off his thoughts, wondering what had gotten into him. Whoever had broken into the house could be getting away while he sat there thinking about how Maggie Arnold looked. Worse yet, whoever had murdered Glen Arnold could be plotting to kill someone else. "Do you have your phone?" he asked again.

Maggie blushed and pulled a cell phone from her pocket. "Sorry. I'm still trying to sort this out."

"Leave that to the sheriff's department," he advised.

Gideon paced the brick patio while Maggie placed the call. He couldn't see any footprints, but the weed-filled backyard was an untamed mess. A crowd of people could have gone tromping through without leaving any discernible marks. When Gideon heard Maggie say goodbye, he returned and sat down by her again.

"They're on their way," she reported, her expression now more drawn than frightened.

"That's good."

"Yes." She looked away from the cellar door and met his eyes. "So tell me. What makes you think my father was murdered?"

Gideon tried to state the facts as simply as possible. "About twenty minutes before I discovered his body, your father called the sheriff's office. He asked to speak to me specifically. You know I used to work for him on the weekends and summers back in high school, correct?"

"That's right." Maggie nodded. "You helped him fix up his rental houses."

"He taught me most of what I know about construction," Gideon confessed. "That's part of why I chose to become a handyman while I'm suspended from being sheriff. Construction is the only thing I know besides law enforcement." He shrugged. "Anyway, your father always felt comfortable talking to me and had called about little things before, so I wasn't even sure this was an official call until we got into the conversation."

"What did he say?"

Gideon shook his head, trying to recall the older man's words exactly. "He said he had something I had to see. At that point I thought it was just some new discovery he wanted me to take a look at. You know, he once found a Civil War musket in a box of balusters he bought at an estate auction. I thought it was something like that from the way he was talking. I asked him to tell me more about it. That's when—" Gideon broke off as a sheriff's cruiser pulled into the bricked parking space alongside the garage.

"I'll finish the story later," he assured her as she rose to her feet. "You don't mind if I hang back for now, do you? I'm not supposed to get involved with investigations."

"Do what you have to do," Maggie said quietly, though Gideon could still hear the fear in her voice.

As promised, Gideon stayed on the swing while Maggie spoke with the officers who'd arrived. He knew Deputy Bernie Gills and had worked with him closely for years. The man had some annoying habits and wasn't particularly professional or friendly when he didn't want to be. But he was a competent officer ten years Gideon's senior, and Gideon had never encountered any major problems with him.

The woman driving the vehicle was someone Gideon had only met twice before—Kim Walker. Kim had grown up in Holyoake but had been a police officer in Des Moines for almost a decade. She had faithfully applied for deputy positions on the Holyoake force whenever any jobs had come open. Though she'd narrowly missed out on those positions, the County Board of Supervisors had chosen her as interim sheriff. The way he understood it, they'd wanted someone new—someone free of any possible ties to the meth production ring that had brought Gideon down. Probably a good idea, as long as she was up to the job of being sheriff.

Gideon sat back and watched while Bernie and Kim split up to check the house.

Maggie returned and sat next to him on the swing. "They're going to make sure there's no one still around," she explained.

"That's good." It was what he'd have done. While he didn't want to judge Kim's work—she'd been rightfully appointed, after all—he still felt a lot more comfortable knowing she was proceeding according to the book. Step one was always to secure the location.

"Do you think I should ask them about…?" Maggie paused, her blue eyes watching him, full of trust.

"About the ruling on your father's case?" Gideon supplied.

She nodded and looked relieved. Obviously she felt hesitant to speak the words out loud.

He understood how she felt. For the same reason, he hated admitting the fact that he was no longer sheriff. Somehow, saying it out loud made it more real. "If I were in your shoes, I'd give them the third degree. They have a responsibility to your father and to you, as well as to the safety of everyone in Holyoake County. If your father really was murdered, then there's a killer out there some-where." He stopped when Maggie looked nervously back at the cellar door.

Guilt stabbed him. He hadn't meant to make her more afraid, but he felt impatient with the sheriff's office for not thoroughly addressing that aspect of the case two weeks earlier. In his mind, it was unconscionable that Maggie hadn't been told the bare facts of her father's case. But then, part of that was his fault. He'd been the one to call her to notify her of her father's death. Not wanting to reveal over the phone that they suspected Glen Arnold's death to be a homicide, Gideon had planned to tell Maggie those things in person once she arrived in town and they'd had a chance to investigate further. But his brother's arrest had spoiled those plans, as well.

Much as he knew he needed to remain completely unin-volved with the homicide case, on a strictly personal level, it was far too late. Glen Arnold had been a mentor and friend. And now it appeared as though whoever had killed him had another mission to accomplish, if the splintered cellar door was any indication.

"I don't want you to worry," he offered, noticing that she'd clenched her hands into tight little fists.

"Too late," she said, her faint smile failing to make the statement a lighthearted one.

"Maggie, can you advise us in here?" Kim called from the first-floor doorway.

"Coming." Maggie hopped up and followed the sheriff into the house.

Gideon leaned backward on the creaky swing and tried not to feel impatient. As he'd reminded himself a thousand times over the past two weeks, there was nothing he could do to help anyone until his case had been decided. If he tried to get involved before then, it would only make things worse. He watched carefully from his vantage point on the swing, but could see little of the inside activity from the backyard.

Letting his eyes wander over the unkempt grounds, Gideon assessed what he could of the setting. The house sat on a large lot just outside of town. There was another older home about half a block away, with a family living there—the Swansons. They were peaceful people, as he recalled. Mr. Swanson was a schoolteacher and his wife stayed home with the kids. If it hadn't been for some large shade trees and the thick row of lilac bushes between the two properties, Gideon might have hoped the Swansons would have witnessed something, but between the distance and the visual obstructions, that seemed unlikely.

The other side of the street was a field of soybeans, while on the left side of the house the yard tapered off into what was once probably a well-kept garden area, though it hadn't been that in eighty years or more. An aging shed marked the rear corner of the property. Beyond that, the wooded hillsides of the Loess Hills sprang up where the Nishnabotna River Valley ended. He wasn't sure who owned the woodland.

As he sat taking in the surroundings, Gideon thought he saw a movement by the distant garden shed. He turned to look just in time to see a light-haired figure disappear behind the shed. The tallish female figure reminded him of Kim. But what would she be doing over there? Had she found a trail to follow after all?

Curiosity overcame his determination to stay uninvolved, and he hopped up, ambling in the direction of the shed. "Kim?" he asked as he neared the spot, not wanting to startle or surprise her, especially if she had her sidearm drawn. "Sheriff Walker?"

He was nearly to the shed when he heard the woman's voice behind him.

"Are you looking for me?"

Gideon spun around. "Oh. There you are." She'd obviously come from the direction of the house—not from back around the shed. "You're wearing tan."

"Yes. It *is* the official color of the Holyoake County sheriff uniforms—" Kim eyed him cautiously "—although I believe the tag calls it *khaki*."

Hoping he hadn't offended her, Gideon tried his best to look apologetic. "Sorry. It's just that I thought I saw a woman—I had assumed it was you—going back around the shed. But she was wearing light blue."

"City cops wear light blue and black," Kim noted.

"I don't think it was a city cop." Gideon stepped back toward where he'd seen the figure, "I wonder if it was someone related to the break-in."

By now Bernie and Maggie had come up from the

basement and approached them. Bernie had apparently overheard much of their conversation. "A woman?" he asked skeptically. "It would take a pretty big person to push through those cellar doors. My guess is you're looking at a good-size guy, maybe two guys. That door was solid." Bernie spoke with an extra-authoritative air, and didn't bother to wipe the smirk off his face when he was finished.

Gideon realized it gave the deputy no end of satisfaction to correct his former boss. And though there was plenty Gideon could have said, he knew Bernie well enough to know arguing with him would only make the situation worse. No, he was in a powerless position now, and he had to behave accordingly. "All I know," he said patiently, "is that just a few moments ago I saw a light-haired female figure walk past here and disappear behind the shed."

"I don't see anyone. Where is she now?" Bernie asked.

"I don't know." Gideon tried to remain patient. He'd worked with Bernie just fine for years—but that had been when the deputy was *trying* to cooperate. The circumstances were very different now.

But Kim was already looking where he'd indicated. "Give him a break, Bernie. He's right—someone was here, probably a woman. We've got footprints."

Maggie was relieved when the sheriff and her deputy finally left. Though she was glad they'd investigated the matter thoroughly, she couldn't get her mind off what Gideon had been in the process of telling her when the officers had arrived. But even as she and Gideon tromped back toward the house, she saw the sheriff's patrol car return.

Deputy Bernie Gills leaped out before the interim

sheriff had brought the vehicle to a complete stop. He ran up to Gideon and confronted him. "All right, where is it?"

Gideon looked confused, and possibly slightly annoyed. "Where's what?"

"My Taser. I left it in the cruiser and you were the only person out here. Don't tell me you didn't take it."

Maggie took a step back as Gideon turned his fierce glare on the deputy. "Bernie, what would I want with your Taser? I carried my own for years."

"Yeah, and you obviously didn't want to give it up when you stepped down, did you?"

To Maggie's relief, Gideon didn't let the argument escalate. "I don't have your Taser, Bernie," he stated flatly. "I don't know anything about it."

The deputy stared down his former boss for several long seconds before he finally said, "I'm watching you, Bromley. Everybody in Holyoake knows you're dirty. It's just a matter of time until the DNE proves it." He headed back to the passenger side of the cruiser and climbed inside, slamming the door as the car drove away.

Maggie watched the marked vehicle as it rumbled away. She glanced back at Gideon in time to see the stern cleft between his brows relax slightly.

"Sorry about that." He looked around them. "I don't know what might have happened to his Taser. That car was within my sight almost the entire time it was back here, except for when I went around the other side of the shed."

"Maybe he just misplaced it," Maggie offered as she led the former sheriff back toward the house.

"Maybe." Gideon sounded unconvinced. "Maybe another officer might, but Bernie's downright particular about things."

Maggie didn't like the sound of that. Between people sneaking around, stealing things and trying to break into the house, she didn't feel very comfortable around the old place. She also felt bothered by Bernie's comment about Gideon being proved guilty.

They headed back down to the basement and Gideon pounded the door frame back into place using long nails from the pouch of the tool belt he wore around his waist. Maggie waited for his pounding to stop before asking him the question that was on her mind.

"What's the DNE?"

Gideon gave the door frame a couple of hard tugs and scowled at it. But the extra nails he'd pounded into place seemed to hold it, and he faced her with a sigh. "DNE stands for the Iowa Division of Narcotics Enforcement. They investigate illegal narcotics operations—in my case, they're trying to sort out the extent of my brother's meth operation, including trying to determine whether I was involved."

"How long does that usually take?" Maggie asked. She could tell Gideon wasn't happy about discussing the topic, but the question had been worrying her. Once his case was resolved, he wouldn't be available to help her. Whether he ended up going to prison or just back to his job as sheriff, Maggie was concerned about whether he'd have time to work on her house at all.

"Simple cases can be resolved in a matter of weeks, sometimes ten days or less. But in the case of my brother's operation, catching Bruce and his men was just the tip of the iceberg. The DNE hasn't told me much, but I know their methods well enough to know that it's going to take a long time to sort out everything in my brother's case, maybe even several months."

Gideon slammed the drop bar into place, then pulled

out his hammer and pounded in a few more nails. His loud pounding told Maggie their conversation was over.

Once Gideon seemed satisfied that the cellar door was secure, he followed Maggie as she climbed the interior stairs. The rooms upstairs were dark, and dusty old furniture filled the first floor, their odd-shaped forms looming like monsters, capable of hiding killers in their shadows, compelling her to quicken her steps as she made her way through the rambling old house toward the front door.

Though it was getting dark outside and the front foyer was dim, Maggie wasn't ready to leave. She had a feeling her questions had already probed deeper than what Gideon had wanted to discuss. But at the same time, she needed to know more about how her father had died. She simply wouldn't be able to sleep otherwise. There was so much that still hadn't been explained.

When she'd asked Bernie Gills about the accidental-death ruling, the deputy had shrugged off her concerns.

"He fell down the stairs. I'm sorry to say it, but he was getting older. Probably wasn't so steady on his feet. And hauling all those tiles, well, a guy has to be careful when he's working alone," Gills had said.

Maggie wasn't sure if she felt hurt because the loss of her father was still so fresh, or if she felt stung because of the deputy's vague insinuation that her father had been careless enough to fall to his death. She didn't like to think that her father was a careless, sloppy man, but then, how else could she explain the mysterious illness that had stricken the people living in one of her father's rentals twenty years before? Everyone had said her father's negligence was to blame. The shame she felt over it was the primary reason she'd left town immediately after graduation, and the reason she still felt uncomfortable showing her face in Holyoake. Facing Gideon Bromley, whose young niece had nearly died from the incident, was even harder.

But right now, Gideon was the only one who could answer her questions. "Do you agree with Bernie's conclusion about how my father died?" she asked Gideon as they paused by the front door.

The stern-faced man scowled, making his expression even fiercer. "I don't like to say negative things about my coworkers, but Bernie had a habit of cutting corners when he could. It doesn't escape my notice that he wrapped up your father's case quickly, right before Kim was appointed interim sheriff. He never appreciated having a supervisor question his report."

"So you think…?" Maggie couldn't bring herself to finish the sentence.

"I think it's possible Bernie didn't want to have to look for a murderer, so he ruled your father's death an accident before he'd fully examined all the possibilities."

It was as she'd feared. "You never finished telling me why you suspected it wasn't an accident."

The formidable man leaned toward her, his dark eyes black in the dying light. Maggie thought about turning a light on, but his shadowed gaze held her eyes, and her fear kept her rooted in place.

"Your father called me," Gideon began again where he'd left off in his story earlier, "and said he'd found something in the basement that he wanted me to see. I asked him what it was, but he said I wouldn't believe it until I saw it with my own eyes. I wish I could recall his exact words, but I know he said it was very suspicious, whatever it was. When I got here twenty minutes later, he was dead."

"So that's the reason you think he might have been

murdered—because he found something suspicious inside the house?"

"Yes. That, and when I found him, his pockets were all turned inside out."

Maggie took a startled step back, and the old floorboards groaned along with her. "Someone searched his body before you got there?"

"That's what it looked like to me. I can't imagine your father running around with his pockets inside out—that just wasn't like him. I knew him well enough to know that. His wallet was lying beside him on the floor, but from what we could tell, nothing was missing. We took fingerprints. Most of them matched your father's, but there were a few that still hadn't found a match when I was last on the case."

Much as Maggie tried to tell herself it didn't make any difference, the idea that her father may have been murdered made his death that much more difficult to bear. She bit down on her lower lip to keep it from trembling.

Gideon obviously noticed her distress. "I'm sorry. Maybe I shouldn't be telling you this."

"No." She sniffled and tried to work her face into a smile. "I'm glad you told me. I was thinking about moving into this house since we're going to be working on it anyway, but I'm not going to do that as long as the cause of my father's death is unresolved." She stopped short as the expression on Gideon's face tightened. "If you want to work on the house, that is. I didn't mean to assume—"

"It's fine. I'll take the job, if you're offering it. I owe your father, you know."

Maggie wasn't sure she understood what he meant. "You mean since he taught you about carpentry?"

"I suppose that." Gideon's mouth tightened into a grim line. "And because I failed to catch his killer."

Not willing to think about that subject any longer, Maggie said, "It's getting dark, and I really don't want to stay here any later this evening. Can I meet you tomorrow morning to talk about plans for the house?"

Gideon nodded and reached for the doorknob, easily opening the door that had given Maggie so much trouble earlier. "Sure thing." They arranged when to meet, and Gideon extended his hand toward her as he thanked her again. "I appreciate having some work to do. This project should give me plenty to get my mind off everything else that's happened."

Reluctantly, Maggie shook his hand, once again surprised by the warmth she felt at that simple contact, and by the glittering blackness of his eyes in the dusky room. "I appreciate your willingness to take on the job, in spite of its complexity." She fumbled over her words as she looked up at him, feeling an odd connection with the man who knew her father so well. With the man who'd found her father's dead body.

THREE

Gideon arrived at the house on Shady Oak Lane ten minutes early and settled his tool belt around his hips where his gun belt used to sit. The weight of the hammer and measuring tape weren't equal to that of his gun and billy club, but it nonetheless felt good to wear the tools of a trade again, even if it wasn't his chosen trade.

He grabbed his clipboard and circled the property, watchful for any signs of disturbance or clues that may have been missed before. It bothered him that Glen Arnold's murderer was still at large, without even so much as an investigation under way to catch him. If Gideon had anything to say about it, the murderer would be caught. He might not be sheriff any longer, but he'd ensure the future safety of Glen Arnold's daughter. He owed the man that much.

As he came around to the front side of the house, he saw Maggie drive up in her father's truck, looking even smaller than usual behind the wheel of the full-size pickup. Poor girl. She looked skittish as she hopped out of the front seat, glancing around nervously as though her father's murderer might leap out of the bushes at any moment. Even from across the yard, he could see the fear on her face, the same vulnerability that had crossed her expression so many times when they'd spoken the day before.

His jaw tightened along with his resolve. He would keep this woman safe. He'd failed her father. He'd failed all of Holyoake County by missing the clues to his brother's drug-making activities for so long. He wouldn't be able to live with himself if he failed Maggie Arnold, too.

"Good morning," he called out so she wouldn't be startled by his approach. "Just thought I'd secure the perimeter before we start."

Her tense expression relaxed slightly. "I appreciate that. You wouldn't think less of me if I told you this place gives me the creeps?" She fell into step beside him as they made their way up the overgrown front path to the porch steps.

Gideon held the screen door open for her as she worked her key in the front-door lock. "Don't ever be ashamed of being afraid. Sometimes fear is what keeps us alive."

Maggie froze and looked up at him. "My father used to say that."

"I know. He's the one who taught it to me." Gideon reached past Maggie, and since she had the door unlocked but couldn't seem to get it pushed open, he placed one hand gently over hers on the knob, slammed his other open hand against the wedged wood, and the door fell back with a shudder. "I should do something about that door," he offered.

But Maggie had stepped inside and was already looking around the great foyer that opened upward to the stud-walled second floor. "I think we've got plenty of other projects that are more pressing."

"Where do you want to start?" Gideon asked.

With a long sigh, Maggie shook her head. She clearly felt overwhelmed by the immensity of the project and all that needed to be done. Not that he could blame her. He'd lain awake the night before, trying to break down the renovation process into manageable steps until he'd lost track of where he'd started. It was such a large house and needed so much work.

"This place will be spectacular once it's finished," he said in hopes of encouraging her.

She didn't look encouraged. Instead, she looked as though the responsibility of transforming the house into something spectacular weighed on her even more heavily than simply making it habitable. Gideon was reminded that he didn't know exactly what her plans were. She'd told him a few things, and he'd inferred the rest based on what he'd have done if the place were his. Those two were likely very different things.

"What are your plans for the house?"

Maggie took a gulp of air. "I want to be able to sell it. My father bought it as a foreclosure after Lorna Creel fell behind on her mortgage payments. From what I can tell, Dad's plans were to convert it back into apartments."

"I didn't realize this place had ever been apartments."

"That was before either of us was born," Maggie explained. "I found some of the history my father had collected about the house, and Susan Isakson, the Realtor who's representing my dad's other properties, let me in on what she knew. This house was built in 1912 as a single-family home, but it was converted into apartments during the Depression. Then in the 1950s Len Turner bought it and turned it into a funeral home."

"That's how I always remembered it." Gideon stepped into the front parlor, arguably the nicest room in the house, though the elaborate wallpaper had to have been several decades old and the wood-inlaid parlor set was worn and rickety.

"He spent his whole career here," Maggie continued. "Somewhere along the line, he hired Lorna Creel as an assistant. She helped with the funerals and took care of the cleaning and upkeep, as well as living upstairs. When Len retired he sold the house to Lorna, who wanted to continue living here."

"But she fell behind on her mortgage payments." Gideon patched the story together.

"Yes. The First Bank of Holyoake held the mortgage, and from what I understand they didn't want to foreclose on her. They gave her plenty of chances, but she refused to talk with them or refinance, so ultimately, they did what they had to do."

"And they sold the house to your father?"

"Yes. He gutted the second floor. I found several of his drawings showing how he intended to convert the house back into apartments."

Gideon recalled from his years working with Glen Arnold when he was younger that the man had a knack for buying up older, unwanted properties and updating them, eventually renovating them into more practical living spaces. Gideon had long been impressed with the man's ingenuity. "And you're planning to move forward with your father's plans?"

Maggie looked stricken. "No." She shook her head firmly. "It always bothered me the way he took lovely older homes and carved them up into cramped apartments. I thought we could just put it back the way it was—a gracious, single-family home."

Gideon nodded and suppressed his smile. Something had lit up behind Maggie's eyes as she stated her plans.

Perhaps she wasn't as afraid of the old house as he'd thought.

"And then you're planning to sell it?"

"Yes." Her eyes bent up at the corners. "I'm selling all my father's properties. The hospital where I work in Kansas City is building a new addition, including an expanded pediatric unit. If I can get fair market value out of what my father left me, I can have one of the rooms of the unit named in his honor. It's been the one thing that's kept me going since his death."

Gideon turned and looked at the room behind him so Maggie wouldn't see his smile. The shy girl he'd gone to school with had grown up into a private woman, but whether she realized it or not, she'd given him a glimpse of what made her tick. Much as he appreciated Glen Arnold's skill in converting old houses into apartments, his daughter's approach more closely paralleled his own preferences. He'd love to see the old house as it was meant to be again.

Maggie's voice echoed behind him. "I know it's going to take a lot of work to bring this place up to code, but as Susan explained it, that's the only way we're going to see any profit."

"She's right," Gideon agreed. "There are probably a dozen older homes in Holyoake that have been sitting on the market for years now, mostly because no one wants to put the money and effort into restoring them. But none of those houses has the potential of this place. It could be…" he let his eyes rove over the walls and tried to envision what it would look like with woodwork gleaming instead of caked with coats of paint "…beautiful," he concluded, spinning around to face Maggie.

Maggie turned her face away before Gideon could see her blush. *He's not talking about you, silly.* She knew he was referring to the house, but there had been a moment as he'd spoken when his eyes had landed on hers with a softness that made her heart catch. *Like Gideon Bromley would ever call you beautiful.*

Gideon had been far more popular than she'd been in high school. He'd graduated one year ahead of her, and while he'd been in the homecoming court and on the student council, she'd always done her best to stay invisible. After all, she knew how the Bromley family and the rest of Holyoake felt about the safety hazards her father had rented out. The people in her father's largest rental house had often complained about strange odors that made them feel light-headed, but her father had never been able to find the source of the poisonous gases. Then, during Maggie's freshman year of high school, several people had fallen ill from the fumes and ended up in the hospital, including Gideon's niece, Kayla, his brother Bruce's daughter, who had nearly died as an innocent toddler.

Pinching back the memory, Maggie turned to face Gideon with a decidedly neutral expression. "I want the house to be safe. Everything needs to be brought up to code. I won't cut corners just to save money. This has to be a house where a person could feel comfortable turning their children loose to play without fearing something might happen to them. But at the same time—" she took in the faded elaborate furnishings, which had once been the top of the line "—I don't want to spend any more money than I have to."

Gideon nodded. "The profit goes to the hospital, correct?"

"That's right." She felt glad he'd followed what she'd said so far.

"Safety first," Gideon echoed. "I'd like to reinforce that cellar door."

Relief filled Maggie at his suggestion. After she'd gone back to the spare apartment where she'd been staying in town, she'd lain awake worrying that the intruder might return. "I think it needs to be barricaded," she agreed. "Obviously the board across the door didn't stop anyone the last time."

"Let's see if we can find something to park in front of it," Gideon said as they headed to the back of the house and the interior stairway that led to the basement. "As I recall there was quite a lot of furniture in the basement."

Maggie let Gideon take the lead on the way downstairs. Though he'd tightened the door back into place the day before, and he'd apparently already checked it from the outside that morning, she still didn't feel certain the house was secure against intruders. But if someone was crazy enough to be lying in wait for them just around the corner in the basement, she was confident they'd get a lot more than they'd bargained for in Gideon Bromley. He didn't appear to be armed, but between the size of his biceps and the hammer he carried, he'd still make a formidable opponent.

To her relief, they made it to the large back storage room without encountering any surprises. Gideon gave a low whistle. "I can't believe all the junk that's crammed back here. I wish I'd had a chance to do more than peek in this room before."

"So you haven't searched through this stuff?"

"No. I'd planned to. Your father said he found something suspicious in this old house, and I got the impression from what he said that it was down here in the basement somewhere. If his death was related to what he found, it might be the only clue we have to go on to lead us to his killer."

Maggie stepped slowly around in a full circle, taking

in the piles of boxes heaped upon old furniture that filled the room. "I think I'll need to move this junk out eventually, anyway. To my understanding all of it came with the house. Lorna acquired it when she bought the place from Len Turner, and who knows where Len got it all? It may have been junk that renters left behind when they moved away over the years before Len even bought it. Some of this stuff certainly looks old enough."

While they'd been speaking, Gideon had poked around the room and now stopped in front of a large armoire piled high with ancient catalogs and other random objects. "This wardrobe looks solid. If we could park it in front of the door it would keep out just about anyone."

The idea sounded good to Maggie. "It looks like it will fit through the doorway. Let's get it cleared off." She plucked up an old paperboard globe that teetered atop a stack of books on the armoire and set it out of the way.

Gideon followed suit, hefting the entire stack of books in one armload. "Do you think you can help me carry it?" he asked from behind the dusty stack of hardcovers. "It looks heavy."

Feeling only slightly injured by his words, Maggie defended herself. "I may be short, but I'm strong. I'm used to lifting children in the pediatric unit all the time." Feeling the need to prove herself, she shouldered a large box, which looked only slightly heavy until she felt its full weight. About that same time she realized she wasn't sure where to put it down.

"Got a spot for this?" she asked, her embarrassment increasing when she realized the strain carried clearly through her voice.

"Here you go." Gideon quickly moved aside some bottles from a dresser top, revealing just enough space for the box.

Maggie staggered in that direction and felt the aging cardboard giving way.

Before she could warn him, she tipped in Gideon's direction and felt his strong arms brush hers as he lifted the crumbling box from her shoulders, depositing it on the dresser before the cardboard gave out completely.

"Okay, so maybe not that strong," she admitted, embarrassed.

"Actually, I'm impressed you were able to carry that thing at all. It must weigh a hundred pounds." He peeled back a loose cardboard flap. "This is full of old window weights."

"Not worth keeping, in my opinion," Maggie determined, brushing the dust from her hands onto her jeans.

"Yeah, I wonder if any of this stuff has value. Some of the old furniture pieces might be antiques, but a lot of it just looks like junk."

Maggie scrunched her nose at him. "I suppose I should sort through it as I go. Anything that appears valuable I can take to an antiques dealer, but the rest I'll just toss. And if I find anything that looks suspicious…" Her throat tightened as she spoke the word her father had used to describe whatever he'd found in the basement—the thing that may have gotten him killed.

"I'll help," Gideon offered.

Though she appreciated his offer, Maggie shook her head. "I don't want to waste your time with sorting through things. There are plenty of projects upstairs that could use your skills—" She stopped midsentence as Gideon's hand touched her arm. In the dank chill of the basement, the brush of his fingers felt warm against her skin. She looked up to see his obsidian eyes glittering down at her.

"If it's all right with you, I'd just like to help. Pro bono. I know Bernie closed this case, but in my mind, there's something down here. I want to try to find it. For your dad." Gideon's voice grew a little deeper, a little huskier, and Maggie wondered if maybe his flint-hard exterior guarded a soft heart. "This project is for the children's hospital, right? I can't take money from sick kids."

Her mouth fell open slightly, and she was distinctly aware of his hand on her arm. Still. Wishing her thoughts would catch up with his words, Maggie struggled to clarify. "You're not going to charge me for the time we spend sorting through the stuff in this basement?"

"No." His tone told her she'd gotten it wrong.

Had she misunderstood?

Gideon continued. "I'm not going to charge you for my time, period. Let me work on your house for free. I'm still drawing pay as sheriff. I can't in good conscience allow you—"

"*I* can't in good conscience allow *you* to volunteer your time and expertise," Maggie cut him off and stepped away. She pulled her arm away from his touch, which, slight and simple as it might have been, somehow felt too intimate coming from the handsome lawman, especially when he was making such a generous offer.

But even as she stepped away from him, Gideon followed her, his broad shoulders cutting into her personal space. She wanted to take another step back, but she was hemmed in by piles of junk on three sides. Gideon looked down at her, his expression far too compassionate.

"Maggie, please. I can't sleep at night. I messed up a lot of things. I missed the clues that should have told me my brother was running drugs. If I'd have gotten here sooner, maybe your dad wouldn't have died. I have enough regrets in my life. Can you just let me do something that will bring me some peace?"

His powerful shoulders loomed at eye level, but what

drew her gaze were his eyes that glittered with unshed tears. Maggie got the distinct sense the hardened sheriff didn't let many people see this raw, vulnerable side of him. Something tugged at the depths of her heart.

The Bromley family had never been churchgoing folks that she'd ever known of. Was it possible that Gideon was facing all these trials without a faith in God to fall back on? She couldn't imagine going through what he was in the midst of, let alone enduring it without God.

His voice rumbled close to her, his tone almost pleading. "If your father was murdered, then his killer is still out there. I need to catch him."

At that reminder, Maggie glanced to the shallow window that looked out on the underside of some bushes outside. Was the killer still out there?

Gideon continued with steady words. "I don't want to frighten you, but, Maggie, your father placed that phone call from his cell phone as he was working in the backyard of this house. In order for his killer to have overheard that conversation, he would have had to have been watching and listening very closely."

Fear trembled through her, and Gideon's steadying hands grasped her shoulders. This time, instead of pushing him away, she reached for him, and let her small hands settle over his shirtsleeves. Gideon Bromley had always frightened her. But her father's killer frightened her even more.

"Do you think he's still out there, watching and listening?" Her question came out as a hollow squeak.

As she watched, the muscles in Gideon's stony jaw tightened and flexed. His determined eyes looked hard. "If he is, I intend to catch him before he can hurt anyone else. Will you let me help you?"

What could she say? She suspected Gideon needed her

help almost as much as she needed his, if the hardened man was ever going to be at peace. So really, the decision was a simple one. "I'd be grateful if you did."

Gideon set to work right away, methodically going through every last trinket and scrap of paper. Much of it didn't appear to have ever been touched—which made it less likely to have been the suspicious object Glen had called him to report. To his relief, Maggie appeared to be just as organized as he was about her approach to the search.

"Do you think this has any value?" she asked, holding up a dusty green bottle.

"I doubt it." Gideon shrugged. "Maybe if you knew what it was called."

"Probably not worth the time it takes to sort it out." She slid it into one of the contractor-strength trash bags they'd found upstairs. "This bag is about full. What do you think I should do with it?"

Looking around at the mountain of things they'd be throwing away, Gideon decided. "I'll hire a roll-away Dumpster. We'll probably generate a lot of debris through the construction process, so we might as well have one on-site."

Once the Dumpster arrived, Gideon was surprised with how quickly they began to fill it. Though he felt encouraged by the progress they were making clearing out the basement, with every bag of trash they hefted outside, he was left with fewer possible clues. Nothing he saw seemed suspicious. He began to wonder if the killer might have had time to remove whatever it was before Gideon had arrived and discovered Glen Arnold's body.

As Maggie toted another bag outside, Gideon's eyes roved over the room. Nothing looked suspicious to him.

Doubts taunted him. Was he pursuing an empty lead? No. Between Glen's final words and the certainty in his gut, he knew there had to be something in that basement. And his instincts had always served him well as sheriff.

"Gideon?" The breathless way Maggie spoke his name from the doorway sent a shot of fear through him. When he wheeled around, the stark-white frightened expression on her face sent his adrenaline racing into overdrive.

"What is it?"

"I think the killer may have returned."

FOUR

Maggie tried to remain calm as she led Gideon back outside to show him what she'd found. If whoever had killed her father really was watching them, she didn't want to give them the satisfaction of seeing how much their actions had disturbed her.

"What is it?" Gideon asked again as they stepped outside.

"I've been tossing the trash into this end of the Dumpster," Maggie explained in the calmest voice she could muster. "I'm too short to see inside it from the ground, but I was thinking after all the bags we've thrown in there, surely they ought to reach the top by now."

She didn't have to say any more. Gideon leaped up the metal-bar ladder that was welded to the side of the roll-away. His groan told her he'd seen the same thing she had.

He looked down at his hands and groaned again. "I suppose I just wiped out any fingerprints they might have left."

"I'm sure they were all gone after I touched it." She tried not to think about what she'd seen inside the Dumpster—the bags carefully untied, the contents sorted out, as though someone had been going through everything they'd thrown out. They may have even been inside the roll-away as she'd thrown in more bags, but she hadn't seen them because of the high metal sides.

But what made her want to scream in fear were the words scrawled along the back inside wall of the Dumpster.

GIVE IT BACK

The jagged block letters made Maggie feel threatened.

"What do they want?" she asked.

"Something from the basement?" Gideon suggested. "It looks like they were searching through the things we threw out."

"But don't you think—" Maggie tried to suppress a shudder, but failed "—don't you think it looks like some things are missing?"

To her relief, Gideon took her question seriously and looked back into the roll-away. "You're right. That bag was full of all those broken vacuum attachments and that old wrapping paper that was falling apart, but I don't see half the vacuum attachments anymore. And I think some bottles are missing from that bag over there."

Maggie could picture the bag he was talking about. It had been dragged to the far end of the Dumpster and all its contents had been emptied out. She knew some of it was either missing or hidden among the other bags. Her gut instinct told her it had been taken. But why?

With a wordless prayer, she looked up to the clear-blue Iowa sky as though God might send her answers straight out of heaven. Instead she saw a broken gutter hanging down from the eaves, and felt that much more disheartened by the project she'd undertaken—which she'd never asked for in the first place. Pushing away her discouragement, she asked Gideon the question that was foremost in her mind.

"Do you think we missed it—the suspicious thing my dad told you about? Do you think his murderer took it with them?" Her voice dropped off as she returned her gaze to the roll-away Dumpster and then back to Gideon.

For a moment she thought the suspended lawman was about to agree with her. But then his features hardened and he shook his head.

"No. It has to still be inside. This only makes me all the more certain."

"Why?"

"Because if your father's killer had what they were looking for, they wouldn't be asking for it back, would they?"

It took three days to empty out the room in the basement. Most of what they hauled out went straight into the roll-away Dumpster, and remained undisturbed after their discovery. Checking inside the Dumpster with every load had guaranteed that, though Gideon had hoped whoever had scrawled the message would come back so they could catch him. Not that there was much chance of that.

They both agreed that, given Bernie's accusations about his missing Taser, they wouldn't bother the sheriff's office about the message, but instead took pictures as evidence.

A few things they found fell into the category of curiosities, and those Maggie took to the local antiques shop for appraisal. But nothing they found fit into the suspicious, you're-not-going-to-believe-this-until-you-see-it category. Certainly none of it seemed like anything worth killing someone for.

After checking the Dumpster one last time and finding

it clear of invaders, Gideon tossed the last contractor-strength garbage bag into the container with a mighty shove, then turned to face Maggie. "Basement—check," he announced, feeling satisfied that they'd cleared out the debris. Only a few large furniture pieces remained, and those they'd agreed to keep with the possibility of using them to partially furnish the house.

When he met Maggie's eyes, Gideon felt his feeling of satisfaction take a hit. That worried look was back, and she'd crossed her arms over her chest as she looked around the overgrown backyard.

He hurried to her side. "I'm sorry we didn't find what we were looking for."

Though Gideon knew she was disappointed, Maggie put on a brave face. "It's okay. We tried. We still have the rest of the house to go through."

"True." Gideon wished he could make his voice sound optimistic. The gutted second floor was wide-open space, with only Glen Arnold's tools and stacks of wood lying around. The attic was a smallish space, and didn't have room for much under its shallow rafters. The first floor was a little more promising, as Glen had hardly disturbed it yet. But Gideon seemed to recall Glen had made his suspicious discovery in the basement. And their pokey perpetrator's search through the Dumpster appeared to reinforce that theory.

Maggie tossed her dark hair from her eyes just in time for the wind to blow it stubbornly back across her face. She let out an impatient huff and tugged loose the fluffy elastic that held a haphazard ponytail at the back of her head. She then finger-combed her hair back and stuffed it into a fresh ponytail. "This pony holder is about shot," she explained, looking apologetic.

Gideon watched with interest. The woman had gone

through the same ritual a dozen times or more each day that he'd been working with her. When she'd secured her hair to her satisfaction, she leaned a little closer to him.

"I just keep wondering," she started slowly, her eyes scanning the yard. "Do you think he's still watching us?"

Though he felt a tiny prickle of fear at her reminder that her father's killer was still at large, Gideon wasn't about to let Maggie see him looking scared. It would only frighten her more. Still, he had wondered from time to time if someone was still watching them, especially when he considered the likelihood that their perp had been in the Dumpster even as they'd tossed bags inside it. "Let him watch," he announced, putting on a brave face. "Now that we're done with the basement, we're going to move on to the rest of the house. So, let's get to it."

They'd discussed the next steps of the renovation process while they'd been working together cleaning out the basement. Gideon had noticed that most of the first-floor storm windows had been installed on the outside of the house, though there were still a dozen more new units stacked against a wall in the kitchen that needed to be installed on the remaining windows. Maggie had agreed with his plan to pick up where her father had left off installing the storm windows. Gideon hoped to get the extra-insulating layer added while the weather was still mild, since the forecast called for blustery fall weather to hit the area soon.

"You're ready to install the storm windows?" Maggie asked, tromping back into the house toward where the units were stacked.

"I brought all the tools we'll need," Gideon assured her. "The wind won't whistle through the windows so much once we get these installed. It should help with the heating bills considerably, too."

"And it will make the house more secure," Maggie agreed softly.

Gideon watched the quiet woman as she reached the spot where the storm windows leaned against the kitchen wall. They'd spoken little during the three days they'd spent methodically searching through the junk in the back room of the basement. Never having been a big fan of small talk, he appreciated being allowed to keep his thoughts to himself. Other than a few remarks about the objects they'd found or a couple of conversations about Maggie's evolving plans for the house, they'd worked in silence. Gideon realized he still knew very little about the woman beside him.

Now she touched the aluminum-framed windows almost reverently. Her fingers paused where the tip of a piece of paper stuck up from between two windows. Maggie pulled it out and looked at it.

"What did you find?" Gideon asked.

"It's the invoice for the windows," Maggie noted, her eyes scanning the page. "Wow. My father spent a lot of money to buy all these windows." Her eyebrows shot up above the upper rim of her dark-framed glasses. "He bought them the same week he died." Emotion showed on her face as she pinched her eyes shut.

Gideon hated for Maggie to be reminded of her loss once again. A thought occurred to him. He wasn't sure if she'd appreciate the sentiment; normally he would have just kept his mouth shut. But Maggie's obvious grief moved him to speak. "It's almost as though he provided what you needed for the house, even though he's no longer with us."

Maggie's eyes remained pinched shut behind her

glasses, and she dipped her head. When she finally raised her head again, she opened tear-free eyes. "Thank you," she said quietly.

Unsure whether she was speaking to him or simply thanking her father, Gideon stood beside her silently for a few moments before clearing his throat and reaching past her for the first of the storm windows. "Ready to get started?"

"Let's do it," she said agreeably.

Gideon carried the first storm window outside. Most of the windows on the old house were the same dimensions except for the large front picture windows. That made installing the storm windows even simpler since he wouldn't have to sort out sizes. He paused in the backyard and looked up at the house. "I'm going to need to fetch my ladder from my truck. Do you think you can hold this?"

"Got it." Maggie took the window, which, in spite of its size, was fairly light. Still, the breeze that had whipped her hair around earlier was still blowing, and tugged at the widespread panes.

"I'll be right back," Gideon promised, and trotted off to where he'd left his ladder strapped to the rack on his truck.

Maggie watched Gideon disappear around the corner of the house. The former sheriff was a mystery to her, made that much more mysterious by his dark looks and quiet ways. His statement about her father providing the windows for them had seemed to come out of nowhere, its sensitivity so much the opposite of what she'd have expected a tough guy like him to say. The man surprised her, and she found herself wondering what other secrets were hidden underneath his granite exterior.

The fact that he'd been accused of running drugs

bothered her. Granted, he'd said he was innocent, and she mostly believed him. But was that because he was really innocent, or simply because she didn't want to consider the possibility that he was actually guilty? After the way he'd reacted when she'd asked him about it the first time, she didn't see how she could bring the subject up again. She felt infinitely grateful for all the help he'd provided, and the last thing she wanted to do was offend him with unwanted questions.

The breeze teased her hair from her ponytail again, sending a thick lock into her face. Unwilling to let go of the window unit, Maggie tried to toss the hair from her eyes. She turned to face into the wind and for a split second, thought she caught a glimpse of a figure at the far end of the lawn. But at that very instant, the wind eddied against the back of the house and spun her thick hair back across her field of vision. Who was in the yard with her?

"Gideon?" she called, feeling alone and vulnerable with her hair blocking her eyes. She tried to toss it out of her way, but the thick locks tangled in the frames of her glasses, refusing to let go.

"Hello?" Her sense of unease increased. Gideon didn't answer. She didn't think he was the figure she'd glimpsed over by the lilac bushes, but she wasn't sure who else it could be. One of the Swansons, perhaps? By then why wouldn't they respond when she called?

"Need a hand?" Gideon's deep voice sounded warm as he dropped the ladder and took the storm window from her hands.

Relieved, Maggie finger-combed her hair out of her eyes, securing it as tightly as she could with the worn-out elastic. "Did you see anyone?" she asked quickly, glancing up at Gideon as he balanced the window unit against the wind.

"No." Concern filled his features. "Did you?"

"I thought I saw somebody over by the lilac bushes, but when I called out, no one answered." She shuddered. "I couldn't see with my hair in my eyes."

"Do you want me to check it out?" Gideon offered, his hawklike eyes scanning the distant boundary of the property.

Feeling silly for seeing things when there was clearly no one around, Maggie shook her head. "If there was anyone over there, I'm sure they're gone now. Besides, the grass is so overgrown over there, it's not as though you'd find anything." To her embarrassment, her voice cut out, a clear giveaway that she didn't feel nearly as brave as she pretended to be.

Gideon obviously picked up on it. "If you saw someone…" He paused and looked sharply across the yard. "What do you think?"

Reluctantly, Maggie admitted part of her concerns. "Remember how Bernie Gills claimed someone had stolen his Taser from the patrol car while it sat here in the backyard?"

"Yes." Gideon's expression was grave.

"Do you think whoever took it is still around? Do you think they might try to use it on someone?" Much as she'd tried to tell herself not to be afraid of whoever might be hanging around, the fact that they could be armed only gave substance to her fears.

She couldn't have been too far off the mark, because Gideon didn't immediately dismiss her question. Instead, his brow furrowed. "That would fit with what we know of our suspect so far. He's been acting in a passive-aggressive manner, avoiding direct confrontation. If he pushed your father from the back, it's possible Glen never even saw the man who killed him."

Maggie tried not to wince, but Gideon's features softened immediately, telling her he'd noticed her reaction to his words.

His hand covered hers where she still held on to the top rim of the storm window as she balanced it upright from the ground.

Forcing a brave smile to her lips, Maggie tried to sound confident. "I guess we should be glad he stole a Taser instead of a gun. At least a Taser can't kill you."

When Gideon failed to immediately agree with her, Maggie felt her concern deepen. "Am I wrong? I don't know much about Tasers, I guess."

Gideon looked as though he was weighing his words.

Not willing to let him walk away from the conversation, Maggie pressed for answers. "How do Tasers work, anyway?"

With obvious reluctance, Gideon explained, "They're fairly complicated. Basically they send out an electrical shock. The kind Bernie carried has barbed electrode darts that can be shot from the gun up to thirty-five feet. The gun can also be pressed against an assailant and used kind of like a cattle prod."

"So it just shocks them?" Maggie clarified.

"The electrical charge is meant to incapacitate the target."

Unsure what Gideon's technical law-enforcement jargon meant, exactly, Maggie pressed further. "Does it hurt?"

"Some jurisdictions used to require officers to be subjected to Taser fire before they could carry the weapon, but with the dangers involved, that's fallen out of practice. I've never been shot with a Taser," Gideon offered. "Reports differ, but there have been lawsuits filed over the years. I discourage my officers from using them, certainly not using them repeatedly because of the risks involved." His voice faded, and he looked as though he didn't want to continue the conversation.

But Maggie needed to know more. It was too difficult to get Gideon to talk about anything. She couldn't risk letting him get away from the conversation now. Besides, if her father's killer was running around armed with a Taser, she wanted to know what she was up against. "So people have been injured by them?"

"Injured," Gideon affirmed, nodding. "In some cases, following repeated shocks, people have died." He cleared his throat and shook his head, which Maggie had already learned was an indication he was done with the discussion.

She'd heard more than she really wanted to know anyway, and quickly picked up on his desire to leave the topic behind them. Hoisting the storm window again, she said, "Let's try to get these in before this breeze gets any stronger. The forecast called for storms rolling in the next few days."

Gideon looked relieved to let the subject drop, and quickly got started.

Glad for an excuse not to think about the Taser or the killer that remained at large, Maggie watched Gideon work, and was impressed at how he was able to handle the ungainly windows as well as his tools, keeping a secure hold of the relatively fragile panes in spite of the wind. She insisted on holding the ladder steady for him.

"You really don't have to hold my ladder," he assured her for the fifth time as he headed up with another storm window. "I'm not going anywhere."

"I feel like I should do something to help," Maggie finally admitted.

"If you think you can carry it, you could bring out the next window. That would save time. We might just get all these hung before it gets dark."

"No problem," Maggie agreed, glad to have a useful job rather than clinging needlessly to the ladder. As Gideon had said, the ladder was secure enough without her holding it. He'd taken great care in placing it in a level spot at a safe angle to the house. And now that they were on the east side of the house, even the breeze had stopped playing with them.

Hurrying around to the back of the house, Maggie hefted one of the awkward frames and carried it back around to where she'd left Gideon on the ladder. "Thanks," he called down. "I'm almost finished with this one. If you want to set that one under the next window, you can bring out the rest for this side of the house."

"Sure thing," Maggie agreed, leaving him.

Inside the house, the stack of storm windows had begun to grow thin. Maggie took a moment to count how many more they had to install, figuring in her head how much time it had taken Gideon to screw each into place. They'd finish the job by suppertime if they kept working at their current rate. Encouraged that they were finally beginning to make some progress on the house, Maggie navigated through the back door with the next window unit.

As she stepped outside, she heard a yell and the horrible crash of breaking glass. Setting the storm window quickly by the door, she raced around the side of the house to where Gideon had been working.

The ladder lay on its side. The aluminum frame of the storm window was bent in a twisted mess over the rungs, while broken glass littered the overgrown grass. Gideon lay on his back among the glass. He groaned.

Maggie was beside him in an instant. "Don't move," she ordered. "Are you hurt? Do you feel pain anywhere?" Maggie could have kicked herself for leaving him to climb the ladder all alone. She'd been in such a hurry to complete the project. Now Gideon had been hurt because of her impatience.

"I'm okay. Just let me sit up."

"Not yet," Maggie insisted. "If you have a neck or back injury you'll only make it worse by moving. Lie still." She carefully brushed broken glass from his shoulders and pinned him down with her hands. "Now, look at me," she requested, trying to see his pupils, since unequal pupil size would indicate he'd suffered a brain injury—a likely occurrence with a fall. Though she'd dusted off the glass fragments from his shirt, the ground was covered with the dangerous shards. She wished he'd be more careful.

"I'm fine," he repeated, turning his head as though preparing to sit up.

"You don't know that." Maggie held his head still with her hands. She wished she could see his pupils clearly, but between lack of light in the shadow of the house and the dark color of his irises, she couldn't see a thing. "I'm a nurse," she reminded him. "I know what I'm doing. You're not getting up until I say it's okay." Maggie pulled off her glasses in an attempt to see his eyes more clearly. No way was she letting him get up—not until she knew he wasn't at risk of injuring himself even worse. She blinked as she peered down at his eyes.

If Gideon was impressed by her credentials, he didn't show it. "Really, I'm fine. All I did was fall off the ladder. How bad could it be?"

Still unable to make out the contours of his pupils, Maggie peered more closely down at Gideon. "My father fell down the stairs," she reminded him. "He died."

* * *

Ouch. Gideon lay still and tried to be patient as he awaited Maggie's assessment of his injuries. He hadn't meant to remind her of her loss, but he hadn't been thinking clearly. He felt uncomfortable with her hovering over him, especially now that she'd removed her glasses and planted her face so close to his.

The woman was lovely. Without those thick lenses, Maggie Arnold was cute, even beautiful, with her pert little nose and the smattering of freckles that dotted her face. And the fact that she had him penned in place, well, he hadn't been that close to another person in years, except for the criminals he'd had to wrestle into submission when they'd resisted arrest.

Human contact felt a lot different when it was an attractive woman who had her hands on his face, holding him down so she could see into his eyes.

Why did she need to see into his eyes, anyway?

"What are you looking for?" he asked, wishing she'd get through whatever she was doing so he could get away, although a small part of him liked the attention and wanted her to stay there as long as she needed to. He felt the need to stomp out that instinct.

"Your pupils. I'm trying to tell if you've suffered a brain injury, but your eyes are so dark," she murmured, her attention so focused on what she was looking for that she clearly didn't notice how close her lips were to his face.

He noticed.

"I have a flashlight in my tool belt," he offered. "If you think that might help."

"Perfect." She smiled and shoved her glasses back into place, quickly locating the flashlight and running through her check of his injuries.

Gideon had hoped the pretty-faced Maggie would disappear once her glasses were back in place, but now that it had been revealed to him, her loveliness seemed to shine through in spite of the chunky frames. She made him turn his head slowly this way and that, and clucked meaningfully with her tongue when he winced.

But finally, after dusting off all the broken glass, she allowed him to get back up, but not without apologizing first. "I should never have let go of the ladder. With that wind—"

"It wasn't the wind," Gideon rushed to explain, remembering now that he was back on his feet and safely away from the delicate brush of Maggie's hands.

"Then what happened?"

"I had the ladder planted in a steady spot right below this next window, and I'd started up with the storm window, but before I got all the way up, I thought I saw a movement below me."

"A movement?"

"That's right." Gideon tried to play back the memory of exactly what had happened. "I was focused on climbing the ladder with the window in my hands, so I wasn't really thinking about who might be down there. I guess I just assumed it was you, even though you'd been coming around by the other direction. This was just off my field of vision, to the right." He shook his head, wishing he'd thought to look closer when he'd seen the movement on the edge of his field of vision.

"So, what was it?" Maggie pressed. "A person?"

"I think so." Gideon swallowed as the memory came rushing back: the lurching ladder, his frantic grasping as he tried to steady himself and the window he held, and then the ladder lurching again as though someone was trying hard to push it over. He'd caught just the tiniest glimpse of the shadowy figure as he'd fallen.

He met Maggie's eyes again, this time not caring how pretty she looked. The situation was serious. "I only saw the figure from above, only for a fraction of a second. But there's no doubt about it. That ladder didn't just fall over. It was pushed."

FIVE

Maggie wanted to call the sheriff, but Gideon insisted that it wouldn't accomplish anything.

"There's nothing the sheriff can find that I can't find," he explained. "And there's nothing to be gained by reporting the incident now. If we find any clues that point to anyone, then we can give her a call. At this point, all we'd probably do is annoy Bernie."

Though she didn't care how annoyed Bernie got, Maggie finally agreed with Gideon. The last thing she wanted was for him to think she didn't trust his judgment. But she wouldn't let him pay for the broken storm window, even when he insisted.

"Absolutely not." She shook her head sternly as she carried the warped metal to the back patio. They'd agreed to remove the glass and recycle the aluminum. "You're already working for me for free. I won't take your money on top of that."

"But I was the one holding it when it broke," Gideon argued.

"It still wasn't your fault. Besides, you could have been seriously hurt. I'm the property owner—I should be offering you some sort of settlement." Maggie still felt guilty that Gideon was volunteering his time as he helped with the house. That he'd been injured while doing so only made her feel worse.

Gideon didn't even acknowledge her offer. "I know you need to watch your expenses."

"Actually, I'm doing okay with money right now," Maggie was happy to report. "Susan Isakson has a buyer lined up for one of my father's other rental properties. With that money coming in, I should be able to afford the rest of the expenses for the renovation."

"That's good news." Gideon looked sincerely relieved. "How soon will you close the deal?"

Maggie finished plucking the last of the broken glass from the aluminum window frame. "We should be able to close this afternoon. I already signed my half of the papers last evening. Susan's taking care of the rest." She handed the metal frame over to Gideon, and watched as he folded the aluminum with his gloved hands. The man was strong.

"I'm glad to hear it." Gideon smiled at her. "Shall we finish installing the rest of the storm windows?"

"I suppose." Maggie caught her hair, which was coming loose again, and secured it more tightly into an improvised twist. "I'd hate for whoever pushed that ladder to think he'd managed to scare us off the project."

Gideon gave her a meaningful look. "I'm glad you feel that way, because I suspect that's exactly what the perpetrator was trying to do."

Rather than allow herself to be frightened, which she suspected would have only made their ladder-pushing enemy happier, Maggie tipped her chin up and said loudly, "Okay. Let's get to work. We can still get the rest of these windows hung today." She dropped her voice and made eye contact with Gideon. "But I'm insisting on holding the ladder from here on out."

"I won't fight you this time," he said, returning her look with a twinkle in his eye.

Maggie's heart did a little happy dance at the look he gave her. She tried to ignore the feeling as she followed him back to the ladder with a fresh storm window, but there was a part of her heart that wasn't about to be easily silenced. Gideon was a good man, and he'd done so much to help her. Why shouldn't that make her feel happy?

While they worked, Maggie kept glancing around, alert to the possibility of the perpetrator returning. She saw no sign of anyone until the sun hung low in the sky. They were just finishing up with the last remaining storm window when a stocky figure appeared around the corner of the house.

Maggie felt a jolt of fear as the man headed toward them, a determined expression on his face. He was bigger than Gideon, heavyset with muscular shoulders under a suit jacket she was sure had to have been tailor-made to fit his broad frame.

"Margaret Arnold?" the man asked as he approached.

"Yes?" Maggie answered, aware that Gideon had finished on the ladder above her and was already on his way down.

"I'm Rex Dunham. Susan Isakson said I might find you here."

"Oh, yes, Rex." Maggie felt relieved to recognize his name. He was the man who'd arranged to buy one of her father's rental properties. "It's nice to finally meet you in person. Did you and Susan get everything taken care of?"

"Signed and sealed." Rex gestured with a thick manila envelope. "I came by because Susan said she thought you still had a key to the house."

"Oh, that's right!" With everything else that had been

going on, Maggie hadn't thought about the key. She had a key ring with all the keys to her father's properties, and she pulled the whole mess of them from her pocket, checking the labels on each until she found the right one.

While she fiddled with getting the right key off the ring, Rex continued. "Susan said you're probably going to sell the apartment house across the street from the one I just bought."

Maggie nodded as she pulled the key from the ring. "Eventually. I just don't have it listed yet." The rental unit he referred to was a large converted house with four apartments. Her father had lived in the apartment at the rear of the building, and she'd been staying there while she was in Iowa.

"As soon as you're ready to sell, have Susan give me a call. I'd like to make an offer on it." Rex took the key from her with a tight-lipped smile. "I'm very interested." His arched eyebrows angled down at her, giving force to his words. "I'll be waiting for that call."

"Okay." Maggie mustered up a smile and stood stiffly, waiting until he turned and walked away before she allowed a shudder to ripple up her spine.

"Rex Dunham," Gideon murmured behind her.

Maggie hadn't forgotten the suspended sheriff was there. In fact, she was glad to have him standing by while she'd faced the intimidating buyer. Now she turned back around and asked Gideon quietly, "Do you know him?"

"A lot of people do," Gideon answered, his eyes still narrowed slightly as he watched the spot where Rex had disappeared back around the side of the house. "He used to play football for Iowa State. He thought he was a pretty big deal, even tried to go pro, but now he's building some sort of real-estate empire."

"He's not into anything illegal, is he?"

"Not that I could ever prove." Gideon turned and lowered the extension ladder from where it reached to the window he'd just finished.

"Do you think I shouldn't have sold the apartment house to him?" Maggie didn't try to keep the concern from her voice.

Gideon's expression softened as he faced her. "Don't worry about it. His money is good—and he has a lot of it. He just won't be the same kind of landlord your father was. Your tenants might not appreciate the change, but then again, they might not notice any difference. I don't mean to malign the man. I just don't like him much, that's all."

"Thanks for the insight. I didn't know anything about him. I've been living out of state for so many years." She followed Gideon to the front of the house, where he stowed his ladder back atop the rack on his truck. As Gideon tied the ladder into place, Maggie asked, "What about his offer on the other house? Do you think I should pursue it?"

Gideon gave the tie-down strap a tug, his muscles flexing as he tightened the strap that would hold the ladder securely on the truck. He seemed to consider her question a moment before answering. "His money's good," he concluded finally, "and you need money for the house and for the hospital. If the deal seems right to you, I wouldn't let my dislike of the man get in your way."

"But do you think it's the right thing to do?" Maggie asked, remembering only after she'd spoken the question aloud that she didn't know if Gideon shared the same set of values as she did. While she was concerned with doing God's will in the matter, Gideon likely considered the legal aspect of the issue as being of top priority.

He nodded down at her, his jaw set. "Like I said, I've never found anything against him. Just rumors and things

I don't like the sound of. If he's into anything illegal, he covers his tracks well enough that you shouldn't get into any trouble with it. If he's got an offer on the table, you might as well jump on it before he changes his mind."

"Okay." Maggie nodded. "Thanks for the advice." For a moment she wondered if Gideon was about to leave. She still needed to lock the house up, but between their project with the windows and Rex Dunham's interruption, the sun was already beginning to set. She didn't like the idea of being alone at the house in the dark.

But Gideon seemed to be aware of her concerns without her speaking them. He looked at the house and the darkening sky, then turned his eyes on her with compassion. "Want me to help you lock up?"

She felt a relieved smile spring to her face. "That would be a great help. Thank you."

They circled around to the front of the house and mounted the porch steps. Maggie spotted a piece of paper stuck in the front door and reached for it, but Gideon's hand flew to her wrist.

"Careful," he said, pulling one of his work gloves from his tool belt and slipping it on before tugging the jagged piece of notebook paper from where it was wedged at eye level between the door and its frame.

With one look at the wavering block letters, Maggie realized why Gideon hadn't wanted her to disturb any possible fingerprints.

GO AWAY

The black-inked letters were foreboding. Maggie looked up at Gideon and met his eyes.

"Who would write that?" she asked.

"How long has it been since we used this door?"

"We've been on the back sides of the house all day,"

Maggie reminded him. "This note could have been placed here hours ago."

"Or minutes ago." Gideon glared in the direction Rex Dunham's car had gone.

Maggie turned her eyes the other direction in time to see her neighbor, Mr. Swanson, arriving home. He waved at the two of them as he got out of his car, and when Maggie waved back, he came ambling over.

"Hey, there, neighbors," he greeted them as he walked up the sidewalk. "What are your plans for this old place? You planning to tear her down or fix her up?"

"Fix her up, if we can," Maggie said, a bit distracted by the note Gideon still held away from him in his gloved hand, as though it might somehow be contaminated if he held it any closer.

Mr. Swanson obviously saw it, too, and scowled. "Where'd you get that? The kids were playing with a note like that in the yard the other day. They said they found it in the bushes."

Gideon's head snapped up at the comment. "Do you still have the note?"

"I think we threw it away." Mr. Swanson shook his head. "I just figured some kids had been playing around. It said, 'Give it back and stay away.' I thought it sounded like the kind of thing kids put on their forts."

"Do you think your children might have written the note?" Maggie asked him.

"The twins just turned four," Mr. Swanson explained. "They're still learning how to write their names. A note like that is far beyond them." He shrugged. "Well, I just wanted to say hi. Good luck with this old place." He waved over his shoulder as he trotted back toward his house, where his twins had come outside to greet him.

Maggie watched as Mr. Swanson lifted each child in

turn and tossed them in the air. "So this isn't the first note," she mused aloud. "Do you think it really was just some kids playing around?"

"What kids?" Gideon asked. "You're on the outside edge of town. I don't know of any other kids any closer than my neighborhood, which is two blocks from here." He scowled at the note he still held.

"Do you think I should call the sheriff?" Maggie asked.

"I suppose." Gideon nodded. "You can ask them to run fingerprints on this thing. I don't know if they'll find anything, but what else can we do?"

"I'm not going to go away just because of some anonymous note," Maggie assured him. She looked past him to where the Loess Hills tapered away into woods. Mr. Swanson and his children had already gone into their home. No one else appeared to be around. So why did she get the feeling she was being watched?

"We're not going away!" Maggie shouted into the wind for the benefit of anyone who might be watching. Then she looked up at Gideon sheepishly.

A smile twitched across his mouth. "Let's make sure our visitor didn't leave us any other presents," he said, giving the front door a hard tug.

As Gideon took the lead checking the many doors on the rambling old house and making sure the windows they'd just installed were securely fastened, Maggie trailed along behind him, her mind swirling with concerns. Who had left the note? Was it the same person who'd pushed over Gideon's ladder? The block letters reminded her of the words in the Dumpster. Or was it someone who still resented her for the incident that had happened all those years before? And what was she going to do about Rex Dunham's offer to buy her father's other house?

On one hand, Rex Dunham's offer to buy another property would give their project on Shady Oak Lane a second infusion of much-needed cash. She wouldn't have to worry about their cash flow at all if the bank account was flush with funds. In that respect, the man's offer was a godsend.

But on the other hand, she wasn't sure how she felt about selling the property—and not just because she suddenly didn't know if Rex Dunham was an honest man. Since all of her father's rental units were filled with tenants, his old apartment was the only place she had left to stay in Holyoake. She'd already been going through his things, though he had little in the way of household items, so clearing out the apartment wouldn't take too long. She could be moved out in a matter of days if she had to.

Which left only one question, but it was a big one.

Where would she go?

Normally she'd have considered moving into the house on Shady Oak Lane. In fact, when she first came to Holyoake, she'd planned on making the move so she could put the last apartment building up for sale. But after all the suspicious activity they'd encountered, and especially after Gideon's claim that his ladder had been purposely pushed over, she wasn't sure she wanted to stay there at all.

Once the last door was locked, Maggie followed Gideon silently to where their trucks were parked at the front of the house.

"You're awfully quiet," Gideon noted as they approached the pickup she'd inherited from her father.

"I often am," she replied.

But instead of agreeing with her, Gideon bent his head a little closer and asked, "Thinking about Rex's offer?"

She confessed with a silent shrug of acknowledgment.

"Why not take him up on it?"

Maggie didn't want Gideon to think she didn't appreciate his concern, so, though she didn't like sharing her thoughts, and especially not her fears, she explained, "I'm staying in that house—the one he offered to buy. If I sell it, where will I go?"

Gideon's eyes darted to the old Victorian and then back to her.

With a nod of understanding, Maggie addressed his tacit suggestion. "Do you think it's safe?" she asked in a voice just above a whisper.

The stern-faced man scowled. "I'm not suggesting you stay here. After that note and what happened with the ladder earlier…"

Not wanting him to think she was easily frightened, Maggie noted, "As a nurse, I've volunteered several times at a free medical clinic that serves one of the worst neighborhoods in the Kansas City area. There've been all sorts of violent crimes committed in the neighborhood, but God always protected us."

At her mention of God, Gideon's scowl deepened. "Don't expect God to keep this intruder away, Maggie. This is a real criminal we're dealing with, even if we haven't seen him." He turned and headed toward his truck.

Maggie tried to bite her tongue, but she couldn't let Gideon walk away with that statement. "God is real, too, Gideon. Even when you can't see Him."

She watched as her words hit the man who'd helped her so much over the past few days, and saw him freeze for a moment, his spine visibly stiffening. She silently prayed that what she'd said hadn't offended him. That was the last thing she'd ever want to do, but how could she have let him get away with implying that God was a figment of her imagination—a fanciful figure like the tooth fairy, whom only a child would believe in?

"I'll see you tomorrow," Gideon called, unbuckling his tool belt and tossing it into the back of his truck.

Maggie swallowed hard and, realizing Gideon would be leaving shortly, headed for the driver's side of her pickup. "See you then." She gave the door handle a tug. "And thank you!"

She looked back in time to see him wave his hand in acknowledgment before he hopped into the driver's seat. Maggie got into her truck and headed off in one direction while Gideon steered away in the other.

While Maggie settled in at her father's apartment that evening, she stewed over what she'd said to Gideon. Had she offended him? Did he feel talked down to? Lectured? She hadn't meant to nag or push her faith on him, but she'd seen and felt God's protection so many times before, not just at the free clinic, but in the midst of critical medical situations. It didn't seem right for her to remain silent while Gideon spoke about God as though He didn't exist.

Finally, after fussing her way through a light supper of canned tuna and crackers, Maggie folded her hands and asked God what she should do. "I know you've protected me through so much, Lord. How can I make Gideon understand that without pushing him away?" Even as she pleaded for guidance, the answer seemed to materialize in her mind.

If she claimed to have faith, she needed to live like it. God had protected her in Kansas City. Why shouldn't she trust Him to protect her at the house on Shady Oak Lane?

Gideon wrote down the phone number, then deleted the message on his answering machine with disgust. He'd been hoping the DNE would reach a verdict on his involvement in his brother's meth operation soon, but it seemed they were just getting rolling. In spite of all the documents they'd already confiscated, they were looking for more information that would tell them what he'd been up to over the past several months.

Throwing himself down on his sofa, Gideon bit back a groan as his bruised body protested the rough treatment. But the bumps he'd taken falling off the ladder that day were nothing compared to what he now faced. He'd given the investigators everything he'd thought would help them—everything. He had nothing to hide, and had wanted to demonstrate that to them. But if he failed to produce any evidence to prove his innocence, would he end up going to prison?

A couple of weeks before, he'd resigned himself to that possibility. But that was before Maggie and the trouble at her house had taken over his heart and his life. He couldn't help her from prison. Someone had murdered her father. He was sure of it. Gideon knew if he went to jail, Glen Arnold's murderer would likely go free.

His failure churned at him, even as Maggie's parting statement haunted him. "God is real," she'd said. Though it seemed like such a simple concept, the idea was new to him.

He hadn't been raised to believe in God. The Bromleys were a self-sufficient clan who'd looked down upon people with superstitious beliefs in God. Growing up, when other kids had talked about their beliefs and religious traditions, Gideon had always felt left out. He'd never had anything to contribute to the discussion. Though he'd been curious to know more, it wasn't in his nature to talk much—especially about things he knew nothing about.

Maggie's beliefs weren't the only thing that frightened

him. She seemed to think God would protect her if she moved into that old house. The thought made Gideon's breath catch in his throat.

Though structurally the house was solid and there was plenty of room on the first floor for her to live, Gideon was still worried she wouldn't be safe there. A week ago, he might have let those worries slide, and figured it was Maggie's choice if she wanted to endanger herself. But that was before he'd gotten to know her.

After spending several days working alongside her, and especially after the way she'd leaned over him that afternoon and looked into his eyes, Gideon had come to care about what happened to the cute, determined woman. There was more at stake now than his usual determination to safeguard the people under his care, whether he was protecting the population of Holyoake County or Maggie Arnold.

He'd started to care about Maggie. That thought scared him almost as much as the threat of going to prison, and the murderer who was still at large.

SIX

The next Tuesday afternoon, Gideon pried up the soft pine floorboards in the second-floor bathroom and looked down with disgust at what he'd discovered.

"Not good?" Maggie asked, obviously picking up on how he felt, though he hadn't said anything yet. He'd already learned she was good at reading him—which sometimes pleased and sometimes troubled him.

"The good news is I found our leak." Gideon pulled at the corroded seal and felt the decaying pipe snap free in his hands.

"Oh!" Maggie's blue eyes went wide behind her glasses.

Gideon looked back down at the rotting floor joists, which had old plumbing tunneling straight through holes cut into them. "The bad news is, this old plumbing job goes against the current code. You can't run pipes through floor joists like that. It weakens them. The floor can actually give out completely if it gets bad enough."

"Oh." Maggie's full lips made a round circle as she looked up at him, obviously waiting for him to announce how he was going to fix it.

He looked back down at the joists that would have to be replaced. This one wouldn't be an easy fix. Not at all.

"What do we need to do?" Maggie asked after a minute's silence.

Gideon shook his head. "For starters, we're going to have to tear out all the second-floor plumbing. That's a big job, but you wanted to replace the old pipes anyway, so it's not unexpected. Then we need to replace these floor joists—that's not a huge deal, either, just that we'll have to tear up the floor."

As he explained the complications of the project, Maggie made a face. Gideon tried not to think about how cute she looked with her lips pursed like that. Instead he focused on what needed to be done with the plumbing.

"Since we can't run pipes through the floor joists, we've got to make a decision. We can either go over them or under them, either by raising the bathroom floor or dropping the kitchen ceiling."

Maggie's distraught facial expression grew more comical. In spite of the dour prognosis on the plumbing project, Gideon found himself smiling at her. "I don't think it's a good idea to make a step up into the bathroom. That's awkward. Our best option will be to drop the ceiling in the kitchen below us."

"How far?"

"Well, we have to accommodate the sewer pipes, so probably a good six inches, maybe eight."

The comical expression on Maggie's face morphed into pinched-face displeasure. "But the cupboards run all the way to the ceiling in the kitchen. If we lower the ceiling, we won't be able to get the cupboard doors open."

Gideon nodded. That was the part of the project he liked the least. Fixing one thing set off a domino effect that required fixing a dozen other things that weren't necessarily broken. "We'll just have to replace the cupboards. They're original to the house and pretty worn-out anyway.

And you mentioned that there wasn't much cupboard space in the kitchen, so that should improve matters."

"But there isn't any room in the kitchen to increase the number of cupboards. If we lower the ceilings, we'll end up with less cupboard space."

She was right. The small, galley-style kitchen wasn't made to house modern kitchen needs. Gideon tromped over to the window and looked out. "We could expand it," he offered. "Extend an addition out the back—there would be plenty of room then."

Maggie's jaw dropped. "How much would that cost?"

"More than you want to spend," Gideon admitted. There didn't seem to be an easy answer to the kitchen conundrum. "What I've read about the real-estate market lately says the kitchen sells the house. With a large, modern kitchen, your house will sell quicker and for more money."

"Enough to make up the cost of expanding?"

"Hard to say."

Maggie made another face. "I'll have to think about it."

"You don't have to decide today," Gideon assured her. "It's going to take time to pull out all these old pipes and replace the joists. And we've got plenty of other projects we can work on, too, before we have to deal with the kitchen."

Her wan smile told him his reassurances were appreciated, though he knew his words were only a small consolation in the face of all that ultimately needed to be done. "This whole bathroom needs to be torn out?" Maggie clarified.

Gideon nodded, already setting to work lifting off the floorboards to expose more of the tunneled pipes.

Maggie grabbed a crowbar and set to work beside him. "What about the first-floor bathroom? Does that plumbing need to be torn out, too?"

Glad to be able to deliver some positive news, Gideon assured her, "No. Those pipes run below the joists in the basement. I took a look at them when we were down there last week. They're newer copper and look to be in fine shape—probably added more recently than this bathroom. The first-floor bathroom can stay the way it is."

"Good," Maggie said, and Gideon thought that would be the end of their discussion.

But a moment later, she continued in a small voice. "I'm going to need a bathroom if I move in here."

The pry bar he was using slipped from Gideon's hands at Maggie's revelation. She hadn't said anything more about her idea to move into the house since their discussion a few days before, and he'd inferred from her silence on the subject that she'd given up on the idea. He grabbed his pry bar from where it had landed on the topside of the lath and plaster ceiling below them. "When were you thinking of doing that?"

"Maybe in the next couple of weeks." Maggie didn't look up from where she worked at the stubborn nails that held the old pine flooring in place. "I talked to Susan Isakson, and she said Rex Dunham's offer on the other apartment house is more than fair. I was thinking about telling her to go ahead and draw up the papers."

"But you can't stay here," Gideon protested. "It's not safe." He'd thought she understood that.

"Nothing more has happened since the incident with the ladder last week," Maggie told him flatly. "The trash in the roll-away hasn't been disturbed any more, no one has tried to break in since we parked the armoire in front of the cellar doors. The house is secure."

Gideon felt his temper rising. Why did Maggie have to be so stubborn about this? And why did he care so much about what she did? "You'd be taking your life into your own hands," he warned her.

"No, Gideon." She looked up at him, finally, and met his eyes with a steady gaze. "I'd be putting my life in God's hands. That's how I lived in Kansas City."

"Well, this isn't Kansas City."

"You're right. It's Holyoake, Iowa. The crime rate is even lower here. I should be fine."

Gideon bit back his anger and pried up a few more boards with a bit more force than was necessary. He told himself he shouldn't care what Maggie did—that if she wanted to live in the house, that was her decision. But he couldn't shake the regret he'd felt at finding her father's body a mere twenty minutes after talking to the man on the phone. If he had rushed right out to the house on Shady Oak Lane instead of taking an urgent phone call, he might have arrived before Glen's murderer had committed the crime.

But then, if he hadn't taken that phone call that morning, he wouldn't have known anything about his brother's drug ring. In fact, his brother's meth lab might never have been discovered.

And he might still be sheriff.

Gideon shook off his regrets. If his brother hadn't been caught, then illegal drugs would still be pouring out of his county, ruining people's lives. He couldn't be sorry for what had happened. He'd done his best. He'd done his job.

A few more of the worn-out pine boards splintered under his anger.

"Are you upset?" Maggie asked, and for the first time

he realized she'd stopped working and had stepped back from where he was muscling through the floor.

"Yes."

"About the floor?" she asked quietly.

Gideon had freed enough space to reveal an entire length of steel pipe. He pulled the hammer from his tool belt and gave the old pipe a mighty thwack. It rattled and fell loose at the seam, raining down bits of plaster, which they could hear hitting the floor below. Feeling a twinge of satisfaction with what he'd done to the pipe, Gideon looked up at Maggie and shook off the bead of sweat that had trickled down his face to the tip of his nose.

"I'm mad at this house," he confessed, sorting out the root of his anger even as he expressed it. "I'm mad that your dad died here, that we have to fix so many things that weren't done right in the first place. I'm mad that you can't live here safely in *my* county, because there's a murderer running loose and I don't have the power to do a thing about it." His frustration at the loss of his role as sheriff boiled into all his other frustrations, and he swung the hammer at another old pipe. The bad plumbing needed to come out anyway, and he figured he might as well attack it while he had the extra energy to hit the pipes plenty hard.

As his hammer made contact with the pipe, Maggie gave a little jump and stepped back.

For a second, Gideon felt guilty for his outburst, especially if it had scared her.

But she didn't look scared. When he finally looked over at her, she had a more determined expression on her face.

"It's not your job to protect me."

"It was my job to protect the citizens of Holyoake

County. I took a vow when I was sworn in, and I meant to uphold it. Your father died on my watch."

"Don't blame yourself, Gideon. You didn't kill him."

"No, but my negligence did." Satisfied that the pipes within his reach were amply broken up, Gideon set to work on the remaining floorboards.

While he worked, Maggie eased her way off the quickly disappearing floor, through the doorway into the hall. He was aware of her standing there, watching him, but he focused on the job at hand and by the next time he looked up, she'd disappeared.

Had his anger upset her? Gideon tried to tell himself he didn't care. Instead he attacked the plumbing removal project with greater energy, taking out his frustrations on the corroded pipes. What difference did it make if Maggie thought less of him? He wasn't trying to impress her. Far from it. If anything, both of them could use a reminder of how very different they really were. They'd been settling into an amiable chumminess that frightened him.

Maggie Arnold was too easy to get along with, and Gideon knew he had no right to get close to her. He was a man under investigation. At any time, the DNE could make their decision and he could be hauled off to prison. It wouldn't be right for him to develop feelings for her. If anything, he should be pushing her away—for both their sakes. He pried up a swath of floorboards, wishing he could fix the other problems in his life as easily as he could fix the old bathroom.

Even if he was eventually cleared of the charges against him, Gideon knew there was no sense in his liking Maggie. She had a job in Kansas City—an over two-hour drive from Holyoake—which she'd mentioned before she was eager to get back to. And perhaps most importantly, Gideon knew Maggie was a devoted Christian woman.

She and her father had always been churchgoing folks, and from some of the comments she'd made lately, he knew her faith was still central to her life.

What would she think if she knew how completely faithless his life had always been? She'd probably be disgusted with him. Everything he knew about faith he'd learned from working alongside her father, and Glen Arnold had been less of a talker than Maggie, so Gideon really hadn't learned much about the details of faith, just that the man lived honestly and insisted on always doing the right thing, even if it cost him.

As he pried the last of the rotten plumbing from the floor, Gideon's mind stuck on the honesty that had been such an integral part of Glen Arnold's life. Had his honesty contributed to his murder? Whatever he'd found, did his insistence on turning it in lead to his death?

Gideon panted from his efforts as he straightened and picked his way back across the exposed floor joists to the door. Glen Arnold had lived his life with absolute integrity. Gideon figured it was time he started trying to live that way, too. Maybe he could start by apologizing to Maggie for his outburst.

Maggie could hear Gideon pounding away on the bathroom plumbing above her. She stood back in the kitchen doorway, unwilling to stand below where he was tearing up the floor above, lest debris come raining down on her. From her vantage point, she could see the entire kitchen—what little of it there was—and she tried to picture how it would look with a lowered ceiling.

Even tinier.

Sighing, Maggie crossed her arms over her chest and slumped against the side of the doorway. What did she think she was doing, anyway? Gideon was right about the kitchen. Nobody wanted to buy a house with a tiny kitchen. What was the point of putting all this effort and money into fixing up a house no one would want to buy?

But the cost of knocking out the back wall and extending the house would likely more than double what she'd planned to spend. It just didn't seem worth it. The kitchen would then be a thousand times nicer than her kitchen back in Kansas City.

Thoughts of home caused Maggie to sigh again. She'd taken leave a few weeks before, and her supervisor had been glad to give it to her, especially considering that she'd rarely missed any work in all the years she'd been on staff at the hospital. She simply hadn't needed to take much vacation. Her father had been her only living family member since her mom had passed away when Maggie was a little girl. And since Maggie hated showing her face in Holyoake, her dad had always been the one to visit her. So she'd be okay to miss work for as long as she needed to.

What it came down to, then, was the fact that Maggie didn't want to be in Holyoake in the first place. Though the incident had occurred over twenty years before, Maggie could still recall with gut-clenching sadness the nasty things people had said about her father after his tenants had fallen ill. They'd called him a slumlord. A liability. Even—her stomach churched to think of it—a baby-killer. But little Kayla Bromley hadn't died. She'd recovered, was an adult now. Not that it made any difference to the people who'd accused Glen Arnold of causing the toddler's near-fatal illness. Neither had the fact that no formal charges had ever been filed against him. In the eyes of the townspeople, her father was guilty, and so was she, by association.

With an audible grumble, Maggie looked at the kitchen and felt the weight of it tying her to Holyoake like an anchor. She couldn't leave until she fixed this house. And fixing the house seemed to get more complicated the more she thought about it.

"Maggie?"

Gideon's voice sounded close behind her, and Maggie spun around, surprised to see he'd snuck up on her without her hearing. She'd been too lost in her thoughts. Looking up at him, she noticed his brow was glazed with sweat and his chest rose and fell with quick, deep breaths. She took a step back into the kitchen and turned her attention instead on the cabinets.

"Sorry for my outburst."

Gideon's apology sent Maggie spinning back around to face him. He'd followed her into the kitchen, and now the little room felt twice as small with his broad shoulders filling it.

She felt her face freeze in a startled expression, and it took her a moment to force words from her lips. "That's okay," she said finally, feeling overwhelmed by the way his masculine presence filled the room. "You said what I'd been feeling. I'm mad at this house, too, for needing so much work, and for what happened here." She cast her gaze down to the floor, as though she could see straight through it to the place in the basement where her father had died.

Gideon must have understood. "There's nothing we can do to bring your father back. I wish there was. All we can do is fix this house."

"I know." Maggie looked up at him with appreciation. "I want some good to come out of this whole mess. I just feel so overwhelmed by everything we need to do to make that happen."

"Renovating a house is like eating an elephant," Gideon noted with an empathetic look. "You have to do it one bite at a time."

"My father used to say that."

"I know."

Maggie wished she could ignore the fluttering she felt inside at Gideon's words and the compassionate way he looked at her. He'd known her father. She had a connection to him she didn't have with anyone else—certainly not with anyone she knew in her life in Kansas City. But that was why she had to leave Holyoake. People knew her here, knew her father, knew what he'd done.

Gideon continued talking. "How about if we break this down on paper? We've discussed a lot of what needs to happen, but I think you'll feel better if we get some of that written down."

"That sounds like a great idea." Maggie was glad to talk about something besides her fears and her father. "Let me grab my notebook."

Turning to where she'd left the spiral-bound notebook she'd brought to keep track of materials they'd need to pick up the next time they went to the building supply store, Maggie instinctively reached toward the spot where she'd left it on the counter.

It wasn't there.

"Oh." Maggie recoiled, glancing around, wondering if she'd set it to the side for some reason. But she didn't see it anywhere. "Did you move my notebook?" she asked Gideon.

"I haven't touched it." He stepped to her side and looked at the countertop with her. "This is the spot you've been keeping it," he affirmed.

"Did *I* move it?" Maggie asked, trying to recall when last she'd had it.

Gideon ran through a replay of the last time he'd seen her with the notebook. "We were talking outside about new gutters. We came in through the back door and you set it down there. I remember because I had to step past you to get a drink at the sink, and I didn't want to drip water on the paper."

"There's your cup." Maggie pointed to the plastic cup he'd been drinking from.

But Gideon shook his head. "I thought I set it on this side of the sink. I'm right-handed, and you were standing over there," he reviewed, a look of consternation knitting the angular features of his face.

Maggie felt her heart start to beat uncomfortably fast. This wasn't happening again, was it? First the disturbed garbage, then the missing notebook—not to mention her father's death. "Is the back door unlocked?" she asked in a dry voice.

"I didn't lock it when we came in. I didn't think I'd need to." Regret filled Gideon's words.

"We've been upstairs since we came back inside, until I came back down just now. Neither of us has been near the notebook since I put it down."

Gideon backtracked into the dining room and spun around, looking everywhere. "You're sure you didn't just bring it with us and set it down somewhere else?"

"Let me check upstairs," Maggie volunteered, and took the stairs two at a time, hoping she'd see the notebook sitting innocently somewhere in the gutted space. Nothing.

Her feet dragged as she came back down. "I'm a very organized person," she told Gideon as she crossed the floor to meet him. "I have to be as a nurse. If anyone's medication was ever to get mixed up, it could be disastrous. I fill my life with patterns and I live by those patterns. I've been putting that notebook on that same spot on the counter for days."

"I know," Gideon agreed in a hollow voice. "Which means someone came into the house and stole it."

SEVEN

Gideon knew Maggie had been upset by the missing notebook the day before, and not just because it meant someone had been trespassing at the house again. Those pages held a lot of the measurements and notes about materials they'd been planning to buy. Now they'd have to start all over reassembling that information. They'd lost a lot of time. And there was a good chance whoever had taken the notebook knew that. There was still something in this house that person didn't want them to find.

Though it couldn't make up for the loss of the notebook, Gideon hoped the surprise he had for Maggie would cheer her up. He made his usual rounds of the house the next morning before Maggie arrived, then retrieved the brown paper grocery sack from his truck. It wasn't exactly gift-wrapped, but then it wasn't meant to be a gift. He wasn't trying to woo the woman. He just wanted to see her smile. Those were two very different things, he assured himself.

When Maggie pulled her father's truck to a stop behind Gideon's pickup, he started to feel nervous about what he'd brought. What if she was upset about it? What if she felt offended? Maybe he shouldn't have brought it after all.

But it was too late to turn back. Maggie hurried toward

the house, and her face broke into a smile when she saw the large paper bag he held.

"That's an awfully large lunch," she said, nodding at the bag. "You must be hungry today."

Realizing the sack looked like a bigger version of the brown-bag lunches he'd been bringing, Gideon chuckled. "It's not my lunch." He stood at her side while she unlocked the door, then reached past her to give the stuck frame its customary extra shove.

As they stepped into the house, Maggie seemed to forget all about the sack he carried. "Do you think we should take an extra security tour?" Her eyes darted from one corner to the next, as though she expected the perpetrator to jump from the shadows at any moment.

"I checked everything outside, as usual," Gideon assured her. "But I'll look around inside, too." He shifted the sack awkwardly in his hands, already feeling self-conscious about his gift. "Here." He plopped it into her hands. "This is for you. I'll start in the basement and work my way up," he said, and made his way quickly toward the back stairs, leaving Maggie fumbling with the sack he'd so abruptly handed her.

When he came back through from his search of the basement on his way upstairs, Gideon saw Maggie perched on the rickety Victorian sofa in the parlor and heard her rustling through the bag. He leaped up the stairs and did a thorough check of the attic and second floor, trying to tell himself he didn't care, really, what she thought of the books he'd brought her. His heart was just beating so hard from darting up and down the stairs, that was all.

"Where did you get all these?" Maggie asked, holding up the home-renovation books and Victorian-architecture catalogs he'd brought her.

"Online," Gideon admitted with a shrug. "They're just

some used books. I was looking for ideas for the house and ran across these. I thought they might be helpful." He still couldn't tell if she liked them or not. Her mouth was twisted into something like a smirk. Was she trying not to smile? Or trying not to frown? He couldn't tell.

Maggie had her face down, looking at the pictures as she flipped through a thick picture book. "Wow." She held open the two-page pictorial spread of an elaborate gingerbread-bedecked Victorian with a corner turret and three-car garage complete with carriage house.

"Obviously some of it is more elaborate that what we'll be doing." Gideon crouched down and pointed to some of the trim in the picture. "But we could imitate this with paint and clever woodcutting and get a similar look for a fraction of the price." He looked into her face and met her eyes. "It might help the place sell."

When Maggie looked up at him, the softness in her expression nearly took his breath away. There was that pretty Maggie again, shining right past her glasses. Gideon quickly straightened and took a step back.

"You don't have to use any of the ideas."

"No, this is helpful," she chirped. "Very helpful. I like doing research. This is a little more my speed than using power tools." She reached into the sack and pulled out the last couple of books, along with the other item Gideon had bought her.

"A ponytail holder?" She looked up at him, and the smirk on her face was definitely an almost-smile this time, as she fingered the fabric-covered band.

"You said yours was shot." Gideon wondered if maybe it was too personal a gift. But he knew she'd been fighting hers for days, and when he'd seen the hair accessories in the checkout-aisle display, he'd grabbed one instinctively. "My niece, Kayla, said that was a good kind for thick hair like yours." Gideon didn't know anything about women types of things, but he watched sheepishly as Maggie pulled the limp old elastic from her hair and replaced it with the new one. He thought she looked better than ever, but when she lifted her face to him, her smile was gone.

Maggie took a deep breath. Gideon had mentioned Kayla, his niece. This was her opening, her chance to ask how Kayla was doing after all these years since she'd fallen ill as a toddler. Maggie had always wondered, and had often prayed for the girl, who she realized was an adult by now. Trying to sound casual, she asked, "How is Kayla?"

"Not the greatest, but she's holding together as well as can be expected, I guess," Gideon said, his stern features grim.

Maggie felt her face drain of color. Her throat felt tight. She'd moved away and didn't know how the girl had faired since the incident, but Maggie still acutely recalled the accusations of several townspeople. The little girl might have brain damage. She might never be normal. Maggie had prayed it wouldn't be so, but if the child had been close to death...

"She's under investigation, too," Gideon said with a frown. "At least her father didn't try to frame her as well, but since she was living in his household the authorities are claiming she may have withheld information. I think she's still trying to sort out what she knew and what she just didn't want to admit to herself."

Though everything Gideon said was in English, Maggie couldn't seem to make sense of any of it. "What didn't she know?" Maggie asked. Did Kayla have learning disabilities as a result of breathing the mysterious fumes? She couldn't figure it out.

"About her father's drug operation," Gideon said patiently. "He kept his labs away from the house, and she insists she never saw anything, never had any reason to think her dad's money didn't come from his transportation company. I believe her, but then again, I believed everything my brother said all those years. I trusted him. And the whole time he was planting evidence to pin the blame on me."

"Oh." Maggie breathed out a long sigh, finally understanding what Gideon was talking about. The methamphetamine production charges. Ever since the way he'd reacted when she'd asked him about it the first day, Maggie hadn't broached the subject, though she felt concerned about the trial Gideon was in the midst of. Now she tried to word her questions carefully.

"What did your brother do, exactly?"

To her relief, rather than walk away, Gideon slumped down in the chair beside the sofa where she sat. He made a disgusted face. "I don't know too many details. Obviously I missed the clues that should have tipped me off a long time ago. And I can't poke my nose into the investigation now—not without putting myself in jeopardy. But I can tell you my brother is a two-faced criminal. He's been producing meth and using his transportation company as a means of distribution. He tried to kill an innocent woman because he thought she saw where he'd hid his lab. When the authorities finally caught him, he tried to put all the blame on me."

Maggie wanted so much for Gideon to be able to prove his innocence. "But how can his accusations stick? Whatever happened to 'innocent until proven guilty'?"

"He's got proof," Gideon said, rubbing his tired face that looked all the more craggy and aged by worry. "He took advantage of my trust to plant evidence against me—fingerprints, a dirty-money trail—just like he tried to plant evidence against other innocent people before me. His claim is that I was the real ringleader, that *I* had blackmailed *him* into doing my bidding."

"But that's preposterous. You were the sheriff."

"Exactly." Gideon's black eyes looked haunted. "He claimed I used my power to cover up the operation—that I kept the deputies away so they wouldn't find the lab."

"Surely he can't prove that." Maggie couldn't stand hearing the dejection in Gideon's voice or witnessing his resignation as he predicted a guilty verdict.

"Conveniently for him, my actions correspond to his story. I received reports tipping me off to a possible drug lab. I was focused on another case and didn't follow up fast enough, and the lab was moved before I got there. My repeated delays meant that I failed to catch my brother. The DEA caught him before I even realized what he was up to. That alone is enough to make me look guilty."

Maggie shook her head, determined to help Gideon find a way out of the mess he was in. She wanted to break down what had happened and find the missing link that would free him. "What do you mean you didn't follow up fast enough? You couldn't get there on time?"

"I was working on another case," Gideon said, his face set like stone, "a case I thought was more important, but which was later ruled to be inconsequential." He shook his head and stood. "We should get to work." He headed for the kitchen.

Maggie followed closely behind him, her mind swirling with what she'd been told. It was like a puzzle, and she knew he purposely hadn't given her all the pieces. And yet…Maggie recalled Gideon telling her he'd lost his job the day after he'd found her father. That was why he'd been the one to call her to tell her of her father's death, but he was no longer sheriff when she'd arrived in Holyoake, so she hadn't learned about the possibility that her father may have been murdered until the day Gideon had arrived to help her with the house. Bernie Gills had ruled her father's death an accident. But Gideon believed it had been more than that.

She stomped into the kitchen behind him, upset that he'd tried to keep such an important detail from her. "You didn't follow up on the drug-lab tips because you were too busy investigating my father's murder." She nearly shouted the words as she hurried after him.

The look on Gideon's face when he turned around nearly caused her heart to stop beating. His dark eyes raged like a stormy night. "Don't think about it," he said softly.

Maggie tried to look him full in the face but she couldn't stand the pain that she saw there. She was right. Oh, she was right. Gideon could end up going to prison because he'd cared about what had happened to her father. And the real guilty parties could end up going free.

"That's what happened, isn't it? You got some off-chance tip about a possible drug lab but you were busy investigating a homicide. By all rights, a murder investigation should take precedence, shouldn't it? How can they blame you for that?"

Gideon shook his head slowly. "Your father's death was ruled accidental. It's up to the DNE to look at all the evidence together. You and I know what we know, but if you look at it from their perspective, it just sounds like a bad excuse." He shook his head dismissively. "Don't think about it," he concluded again.

But Maggie was still thinking about it, and she'd reached another conclusion—one that gave her hope. "But if we find my father's killer, if we can prove he was murdered, then no one can say you weren't right for dealing with the events the way you did. Right?"

A weak smile eased its way across Gideon's stony face. "It wouldn't clear away all the charges, but it might tip the scale back in my favor." He pulled the measuring tape from his tool belt. "Now can we drop the subject and get back to work?"

Maggie gave a satisfied nod, though she still had plenty of questions—including the unanswered issue of whether Kayla had fully recovered from her illness. But Gideon was clearly done talking and Maggie didn't think she could handle another heavyweight discussion at the moment, anyway. She'd lived with uncertainty about Kayla for the past twenty years. She could wait to ask Gideon until he gave her another opportunity to talk.

Maggie felt a little sheepish when she arrived at the house the next day with a fat pad of graph paper filled with drawings. Inspired by the books Gideon had given her, she'd been up half the night sketching out ideas for the house. Twice she'd tried to go to bed and had instead lain awake thinking about walls and doors and room layouts until she'd had to switch the light on again and commit her ideas to paper before she could sleep.

She stifled a yawn as Gideon gave the front door its customary extra shove to let them both inside. While Gideon did a quick check to make sure the interior was secure, Maggie said a quiet prayer that he'd like the ideas she'd sketched up. She didn't know much about construction, so she had no idea if the room layouts were even workable, but she trusted Gideon's expertise to fill in the gaps.

"Don't worry," Gideon said as he clomped down the front stairs in his thick work boots. "The house is secure." It had become part of their morning ritual for Gideon to check the house, but Maggie didn't want the precaution to become so routine that they let their guard down. Her father's killer could return at any time.

"I trust you," she assured him, and then shoved the real cause for her anxiety toward him as he met her in the foyer. "I looked at the books you bought," she explained, handing him the thick tablet that contained her ideas. "I drew up some rough sketches—I don't know if they're any good."

"Let's take a look at them," Gideon offered, and moved into the parlor to sit at one end of the old sofa.

Maggie thought about sitting in the chair beside the couch, but she realized she'd be too far from him then to see the drawings and explain them. Hesitantly, she perched near him on the couch. Pointing at the drawings he held, she began, "This is north. Here's the wide front window." Then she launched into a detailed description of everything she'd drawn, going through the pages and describing what the precise lines and notations meant.

At first Gideon scowled at the pages, and Maggie wasn't sure if he was skeptical of her plans or if he was simply concentrating. But he quickly started asking questions and clarifying—he seemed to take her efforts seriously, which increased her confidence as she approached some of the less obvious choices she'd made.

"I thought we could move the hall bath to where dad had roughed in an upstairs apartment kitchen," she suggested, her hands brushing his as she pointed to where she'd drawn the bathroom sink. "We could fit a double vanity along this wall. People like those. It might help the house sell."

"So this would be a master bathroom." Gideon picked up on how she'd connected the bathroom to the biggest bedroom she'd drawn. Though his brow was furrowed, he didn't look so much dubious as intent. His words encouraged Maggie to continue.

Nodding, she explained, "One of the books spent a whole chapter talking about how master suites are a big selling point in today's market. I thought since our walls aren't in yet anyway, we could use this configuration to increase the house's selling value without really changing our total costs."

"I like that. You could even make the closet larger like this," he said, grabbing the pen she'd clipped to the notepad and flipping through the pages, obviously looking for a blank sheet to draw on.

Maggie reached to direct his search, but before she caught him, he'd flipped to the back pages she hadn't intended him to see.

"What's this?"

"Nothing." Maggie felt the color rise to her cheeks. She tried to cover the pages, but the touch of Gideon's fingers stalled her hands. "I didn't mean—" she began.

But Gideon interrupted her excuses. "This is an expanded kitchen," he observed quickly. "You've added an eat-in island with a sink."

"I saw a picture in one of the books." Maggie shook her head, wishing she'd thought to tear out those pages before she'd handed over the notebook. "But I didn't intend—"

"This is good. You've got your oven here." Gideon blatantly disregarded Maggie's fumbling efforts to pull the papers away from him. "*Two* sinks, then, hmm?" He cast her a look as though she'd been up to some sort of mischief.

Maggie felt her blush deepening. "The resale value," she began, but Gideon cut her off.

"This is excellent. I'll run an estimate on what you have drawn here."

"Gideon," she said in her most authoritative voice. She had to end this charade immediately. "I have no intention of bumping out the kitchen. It was just an idea I had, just supposing. We're not really going to pursue it."

But the lawman's craggy features softened to a smile. "It's a good idea. I really think you should think about it. I'll get some numbers to you, then you can decide."

"I don't want to waste your time—" Maggie protested.

Gideon simply smiled at her. "Then don't ask me to build a worthless, tiny kitchen." He tore out the page she'd drawn. "I'll make a copy of this and get those numbers for you as soon as I can."

For the rest of the day, Gideon had to force himself to stop smiling. He liked Maggie's ideas. More than that, he liked that she cared enough about the project to brainstorm so much about what they could do with the marvelous old house. And he felt encouraged that he might eventually be able to convince her to expand the kitchen, which he was certain was a necessary step toward restoring the old house to its maximum potential.

While they worked together with the kitchen demolition that was a necessary step no matter how they decided to proceed with the space, Gideon thought about possibilities of how they could reconstruct the room. Guiltily, he realized he was picturing himself working alongside Maggie preparing a meal in the finished kitchen.

Obviously, the mental image was prompted by the fact that he was working beside her tearing out the old kitchen. And because of the discussions they'd had about how the space would ultimately function. The images were simply hypothetical. They had no grounding in reality. He couldn't let himself read too much into them.

When Maggie's cell phone rang at three o'clock, Gideon tried not to listen in on her conversation, but he couldn't ignore the sheet-white expression on her face as her mouth bent into that innocently cute pursed-open expression. Something was up.

"What is it?" he asked, dropping the crowbar he'd been wielding as Maggie closed the phone.

Looking shaken, Maggie leaned back against the last remaining section of countertop. "That was Susan Isakson," she said, her blue eyes wide as she looked up at him. "I had told her to turn down Rex Dunham's offer on the apartment house I'm staying in. He called her back with a counteroffer."

Gideon felt her words close over him like a trap. If Maggie sold the apartment house, she'd have little choice but to move into the Victorian. He had strong reservations about her safety there. "It's not really my place to ask what the offer was," he admitted.

Maggie pressed her hands to her temples and shook her head slowly. When she next spoke, her voice had gone up half a squeaky octave. "He raised his offer another twenty thousand dollars."

"Twenty thousand," Gideon repeated, though he'd heard her clearly. "That's—"

"Enough to pay for the difference in kitchen plans if we decided to expand," Maggie said, meeting his eyes with fear and doubt clouding her expression. She had obviously thought the offer through while she'd been on the phone with Susan.

The happiness he might have otherwise felt at hearing her consider the expansion was clouded over by what such a move would mean.

"Would he let you continue living in the rear apartment?"

Maggie shook her head. "According to Susan, Rex has a potential tenant all lined up. That's part of why he's so eager to get his hands on the house. He doesn't want to lose this renter. Dad's apartment is really nice. He's tinkered with it so much, adding built-ins and trying out new features. Rex thinks he can charge a premium for the space. I'm sure he's right."

"Where will you go?" Gideon asked, trying to deny how important her answer really was to him.

"What choice do I have? I'll have to stay here. Or else…"

Gideon braced himself, but he still wasn't prepared for how much her next words stabbed at his heart.

"I'll have to go back to Kansas City."

EIGHT

After he got home that evening, Gideon took out some of his frustration on the punching bag in his basement. The weighted bag thumped around like a rapidly beating heart, but it couldn't match the rhythm his own heart pulsed with.

He told himself it didn't matter what Maggie did. She should go back to Kansas City. It was where she lived. It was where she belonged. And it was plenty far enough away from him and all his troubles.

The thoughts were straight in his head, but with every tearing thump of his heart, he knew he still didn't like it. Was it selfish of him to want to keep Maggie around? She kept his mind off the investigation against him. And whenever they *had* spoken about that issue, she'd vehemently defended him. No one else had done that.

Besides that, the perky little woman was fun to work with. She didn't jabber too much like most women he knew. She didn't boss him around or shy away from hard work. She hadn't even gotten too spooked when he'd lost his temper tearing out the bathroom. Maggie Arnold was good for him.

But that didn't change the fact that he was absolutely no good for her. She was a Christian. He didn't know anything about having faith. She lived in the city. He belonged in Holyoake. And even if there was some way past all their other differences, there was the glaring fact that he'd likely soon be carted off to prison for a long, long time. There was certainly no way he could let on to his growing feelings for her, let alone act on those feelings. It simply wouldn't be fair to her.

Ultimately, he knew that, much as he might have liked to ask her to find another place to stay in Holyoake, he didn't have any say in the matter. What Maggie decided would be up to her. He'd just have to learn to live with it.

Leaning exhaustedly against the punching bag, Gideon tried to straighten out his thoughts, which kept swirling around the house and Maggie and her father, who'd died there. Glen Arnold had been a father figure to him. Since Gideon had been born when his parents were relatively old, his own father had been more like a grandparent and his older brothers had been like, well, like bossy older brothers.

But Glen Arnold had taught him things no one else had, and not just about carpentry.

Since he was in his basement already, Gideon left the punching bag and rummaged through a stack of boxes that held things he had never unpacked after moving into his one-bedroom bungalow. The Bible was right where he'd packed it, next to a bunch of his old textbooks from college.

Glen Arnold had given him the leather-bound volume as a graduation gift. Gideon hadn't known what to do with it, but he flipped it open to the page in the middle that Maggie's father had marked with a bookmark.

The bookmark had his name on it, along with the biblical meaning: "mighty warrior." Gideon smiled. He'd liked that image when he'd first read it, fresh out of college and ready to fight for justice. Now he felt a little disillusioned when he saw the words.

Glancing at the pages the name card marked, Gideon reread the words Glen Arnold had underlined, their meaning less obvious to him now than they had been when he'd first read them years before.

Unless the Lord builds the house, its builders labor in vain.

What did that mean? Obviously it was a reference to working construction. Glen Arnold had taught him everything he knew about that. But *they'd* been the builders, not the Lord. Hadn't they?

Gideon carried the book upstairs with him, wondering if he could possibly ask Maggie about what the verse meant. But then she'd realize how ignorant he was. Maybe all Christians were supposed to understand that stuff. It was just another reminder of how he and Maggie lived in two completely different worlds.

He tried to put the issue out of his mind, but the words seemed to stick in his head. *Unless the Lord builds the house, its builders labor in vain.* Did that mean all their efforts at rebuilding the house on Shady Oak Lane were futile? Maybe he needed to get God on board somehow. Gideon looked at the thick book with its tiny lettering and wondered if there was any chance the answer was on one of those pages. Since he didn't know where else to turn, he sat down and started reading.

Maggie arrived at the house on Shady Oak Lane extra early the next morning, and sat in her father's truck praying while she waited for Gideon to arrive. She'd solidly made up her mind, but she knew Gideon wouldn't agree with the conclusion she'd reached. Still, there didn't seem to be any way around it.

After calling Susan again the evening before and quizzing her on possible places to stay, Maggie was even more convinced she had no other choice in the matter. As Susan had explained it, the real-estate market in Holyoake had gotten caught up in the same troubles that plagued the national scene. In the wake of the foreclosure crisis, there was a glut of unwanted houses on the market, but a massive shortage of rentals, especially in such limited space as Holyoake. That was part of why Rex was so eager to get his hands on her father's house. Susan didn't know of a single place in Holyoake where Maggie could rent a room, and certainly not on short notice. So that was that.

As Gideon arrived and completed his security check of the grounds and house, Maggie asked him solemnly, "Any sign of disturbance?"

"Not this morning." He held her gaze as he reported his findings. "Even the bags in the roll-away are just as we left them."

"Good. So it's been over a week since we've had any sort of incident."

"You're not still thinking of moving in here, are you?"

Maggie didn't see as much anger in his response as she'd feared he might have. She knew how strongly he felt about protecting the citizens of Holyoake County—even if she technically wasn't a resident. "I talked to Susan about my options last evening. She said I could accept Rex's offer on the apartment and close in two weeks. That would give me time to finish clearing out Dad's apartment and get a room ready for me to move in here. I've decided if anything frightening happens at this house in the next two weeks, I won't move in. But if the next two weeks pass without incident, I'll assume it will be safe for me to live here."

She spoke with a confidence she didn't really feel, but was relieved when Gideon didn't protest her proposal, though the furrow in his brow had deepened and his eyes were even darker than usual. He still didn't look very happy about it.

"A lot can happen in two weeks. Are you saying if anything else gets stolen or broken into, you'd back out of the sale?"

Maggie gave a small shrug in response. "Depending on what the incident was, I'd probably just go back to Kansas City. As long as you're still able to work on the house, I should be able to make most decisions over the phone."

Gideon nodded gravely, and Maggie felt relieved. So far, so good. The next two weeks would determine what would happen.

Almost against his better judgment, Gideon made tremendous progress on the house over the next two weeks, including finishing the first-floor den into a cheery bedroom space complete with locking door for added security. He had insisted on that part.

He wasn't sure whether to feel disappointed or relieved, but there were no further incidents at the house on Shady Oak Lane. Fall hit the region with a vengeance, and it was a blustery day when he helped Maggie cart over the last of her things so she could stay the night at the house.

"You've got my cell-phone number on speed dial," he confirmed again before he left for the evening. "I'm only two blocks away. Don't hesitate to call no matter what time it is. Even if you just get a bad feeling about something. You'd be surprised how many victims of violent crimes said they had a gut feeling something was wrong beforehand."

"I'll be okay," Maggie assured him. "I plan to keep a crowbar next to my bed. If anyone attacks me, I'll whap them with it." The laughter in her eyes told him she was joking, though knowing her, she'd probably still have the crowbar on her nightstand.

Unsure whether he was acting overprotective, Gideon scowled at her remark. "I'm still not crazy about this idea."

"You think I'm the crazy one," Maggie said, looking up at him, all sign of joking gone from her eyes.

Wow. The purity and trust in her frank expression hit him like an arrow to his heart. If he hadn't already known he had a weakness for this woman, he would have realized it then. Instead, the realization simply reinforced his determination to keep his growing feelings hidden. Maggie had enough trouble to deal with, between the house and the loss of her father. She didn't need to get entangled with the messes in his life.

Gideon deepened his scowl. "You're a grown woman. You can do as you wish. I've given my honest assessment." He broke off before the strain he felt carried through to his voice. Stepping away from her, he said gruffly, "I'll lock the door on my way out."

"I appreciate that. Good night."

"'Night."

Boom! Thump!

The noise woke Maggie from a deep slumber. After three uneventful nights staying in the old Victorian, she'd overcome her fear enough to sleep soundly—but not too soundly to hear the thumping and banging that echoed through the house.

Maggie fumbled for the cell phone on her nightstand and heard it hit the floor with a clunk that sounded tiny in comparison to the booming sounds that filled the house. The noises were coming from the rear, near the kitchen. And below. Someone was trying to break in through the cellar door again!

Hopping from the bed and scrambling with her hands on the old plank floor, Maggie hit the phone with her fingers in the darkness and sent it skittering farther under the bed. Did she dare turn on a light to find it? She doubted she'd locate it in time if she didn't.

Thump! Scrape!

The light from the bedside lamp filled the room as Maggie all but dived under her bed and snatched up her phone, flipping it open and sending a call to Gideon before she even saw what time it was. She pulled on her glasses and looked at the clock. Four in the morning? Would Gideon even hear her call at such an early hour?

Boom!

"Hello?" Gideon's sleep-deepened voice had never sounded so good, and Maggie felt her heart give a grateful cry.

"Someone's breaking in the cellar door."

"I'll be there in two minutes. Hide."

Thump!

The call went dead. Maggie assumed Gideon had closed his phone to throw on shoes so he could race over. She knew his house was only a couple of blocks away, and she wondered if he'd try to drive over or simply strike out on foot. Driving would be faster, but louder. What if he frightened the intruder away?

Boom! Scrape!

She could hear the heavy armoire scraping the floor as the intruder pushed back the door. The solid piece of furniture was heavy—so heavy she and Gideon combined had barely been able to lift it. It would take a mighty strong man to move it away from the door.

Thump! Scrape!

Recalling Gideon's instructions that she hide, Maggie flipped off the light and dived under the bed, pulling down the edges of her bedding to camouflage her presence.

Thump! Scrape!

Boom! Scrape!

Maggie didn't know how far the old armoire was moving with each blow, but the intruder surely wouldn't need to push it much farther before he gained entry.

Thump! Scrape!

The sound of a revving engine was nearly obscured by the echoing booms from the basement. Maggie hoped the perpetrator wouldn't hear Gideon coming so the suspended sheriff could catch him in the act.

But what if the man was armed? He could injure Gideon! "Lord, protect Gideon, *please!*" Maggie whispered the prayer repeatedly, realizing only after some time had passed that both the sound of the engine and the sounds of the intruder had stopped. Silence pressed in on her hiding place under the bed, and the darkness hid whatever was happening outside. So much time had passed. Where was Gideon?

Cautiously, Maggie crawled out from under the bed and pulled on clothes and shoes. She grabbed the ponytail holder Gideon had given her and tiptoed toward the bedroom door. She thought she heard a key scraping in the front-door lock. That would have to be Gideon—he was the only person besides herself who had a key to the house.

Footsteps padded softly down the hall to her door, and she heard a gentle rapping on the other side.

"Maggie? Are you okay?"

Before Gideon finished his sentence she had the door open, and in her relief at seeing him unharmed, she nearly threw herself at him. Fortunately she retrained herself before she did anything embarrassing. He must have read the questions on her face.

"He got away." Gideon shook his head regretfully. "I shouldn't have driven over. He heard me coming and headed for the woods. I tried to give chase but I lost him in the trees."

"It's okay." Maggie didn't want Gideon to blame himself, especially when she felt so relieved he hadn't been hurt. "If you hadn't arrived as quickly as you did, he might have gotten inside." She knew her fumbling with the phone had also cost them valuable time.

"Do you think he might have actually made it past the armoire?" Gideon asked.

"I think he very nearly did. It sounded like he was throwing his body weight against it, and it kept scraping against the floor like he was moving it. I thought for sure at any second he'd come inside."

As she spoke, Gideon's features clouded and he reached for her arm, guiding her gently but firmly back into the room. "Call the sheriff. Now," he whispered with urgency as he turned and locked the door after them. Then he crossed the room and switched off the light.

Maggie did as she'd been told, her heartbeat kicking up rapidly as she completed the emergency call. When the dispatcher assured her that help was on the way, Maggie thanked the woman and closed the call. In the darkness it was difficult for her to see Gideon, but she felt his presence near her.

"I thought you said you chased him into the woods."

"I chased one man. We don't know if he was working

alone. If the cellar door has been compromised anyone could have gotten into the house."

Maggie responded to the sound of Gideon's voice by reaching for him instinctively, placing a tentative hand on his arm. She'd come to depend on this man, and the feel of his warmth and the strength that radiated through the lightweight fabric of his shirtsleeve brought her a comfort she hadn't known she needed to feel. She had to resist the urge to lean on him any more than she already was.

Silent seconds ticked by, and Maggie wondered what the likelihood was that an intruder was in the house with them. Perhaps it was foolish, but she didn't feel nearly as afraid now that Gideon was with her. In fact, she felt a twinge of disappointment when she heard the sound of approaching sirens.

Gideon stepped away from her and switched the light back on.

"Are you coming with me?" Maggie asked quietly.

"I need to give them a description of the man I chased through the woods."

His words reminded Maggie that she still hadn't heard what the perpetrator had looked like. Once outside, she listened to Gideon describe their suspect to the deputy who arrived on the scene.

"He had his back to me the whole time, so unfortunately I never saw his face. But he was a big guy, not exceptionally tall, but wide through the shoulders and chest. A fifty-two coat size, maybe bigger."

"Heavyset?" the officer clarified. To Maggie's relief, it was a kind-looking older man, and not Bernie Gills, the deputy who'd accused Gideon of stealing his Taser.

"I wouldn't say so, no." Gideon's face scowled in a way Maggie had come to recognize as a look of concentration more than one of displeasure. "He had to have been in pretty good shape. He was fast and agile on his feet. He darted around the trees in the woods with no trouble at all. I tried to follow the sound of his running, but he must have hid from me, because in the end there wasn't any sign of him, no sight or sound. I didn't want to give up the search, but I simply had nothing to go on, and the last thing I wanted to do was trample any footprints he might have left us. With the rain we had last week the ground should still be soft enough to pick up some prints, especially in that loess soil."

The deputy offered to return after daylight and try to pick up a trail in the woods, but Gideon assured him he'd take care of searching, and that he'd call the sheriff's office if he found anything suspicious. After searching the house and finding nothing that would indicate anyone had come inside, the deputy left with their statements. By that time the faint pink predawn had begun to creep up in the east, and bats swirled in circles high in the sky above them, returning to their nests after a night of hunting. Maggie shivered as she turned to face Gideon in the chill of the backyard.

"Can I make you some coffee?" she asked him, knowing well enough from having worked with him over the past few weeks how he liked his brewed.

"You do that." Gideon nodded and stepped toward the house. "I'm going to search the inside of the house again. There are too many places where someone could hide. It's not that I don't trust the deputy—" he cast a glare toward the woods "—I just don't trust our perp."

Gideon smelled the welcome aroma of rich coffee as he made his way toward the kitchen with heavy feet. The man had gotten away. Again.

"I should have come on foot," he said with regret as he took the steaming mug Maggie handed him.

"No." The little woman shook her head so forcefully the ponytail at the back of her head gave an emphasizing shake of its own. "That would have taken too long. I'm glad he heard you coming. If you'd caught him by surprise, who knows what might have happened. If he was armed—"

"I'm trained to deal with armed men. As it is, he got away."

"But at least we have a description of him."

"We have a description of his back," Gideon countered. "You can't ID a suspect based on the width of his shoulders alone."

"Yeah, but how many people with shoulders that broad can dart quickly through the trees? He sounds like a football player to me."

Gideon had thought of that, but didn't want to frighten Maggie with his theories. Besides, he didn't want to name any names before they had any more evidence.

Apparently Maggie had no such qualms. "Ever wonder why Rex Dunham is so eager to get his hands on my father's properties?"

"He closed on the other house three days ago. Why would he come here?"

Maggie sipped her coffee with a thoughtful look before answering. "You said my father found something suspicious in the basement, and that his pockets had been searched before you found him. I don't think the thing the killer was looking for was in his pockets. Obviously he's still looking for it. That's why he searched the trash in the roll-away Dumpster, but he didn't find it there, either. He had to give up once he realized we'd discovered what he'd been doing."

Gideon nodded along with her theory, but he had his doubts. "That still bothers me. Why would he search the Dumpster when we were on-site? We could have caught him at any moment."

After a thoughtful pause, Maggie shuddered and met his eyes. "Perhaps he figured if we caught him, he could just kill us, too." Her voice rose a frightened half octave. "If Rex killed my father to get his hands on something but he didn't find it here, maybe he figured my dad had taken it back to his apartment. And now that he's had three days to search there, he's decided it must be here after all."

The fear and the pain on Maggie's face were too much for Gideon to see. He couldn't let her dwell on suspicious theories. They had to do something. "If this guy thinks something is still in the house, then maybe it is. Where haven't we looked yet?"

"The second floor is wide-open space, except for the chimney, and I guess, the floorboards. So I think we can rule that out." As she worked toward solving the problem, a calm seemed to come over Maggie, and she grabbed up the new notebook she'd started using ever since the last one had disappeared. "That leaves the first floor and attic," she said, jotting notes.

Gideon liked the new direction their conversation was going. They'd search methodically, slowly going over the whole house. It was what he was good at. And they could search everything at their leisure. At least they had that much advantage over their would-be intruder. "We've already checked the basement. There's nothing down there but a few pieces of furniture, and we thoroughly searched those, too."

"The attic really isn't that big," Maggie noted, "though it does have some old furniture and junk in it."

"But your father never mentioned the attic."

"And the intruder keeps trying to come in through the basement. You'd think if he wanted in the attic he'd climb the trellis onto the porch roof and break in through a window."

"So let's rule out the attic for now." Gideon watched with satisfaction while she drew a line through that entry in her notebook. "That leaves the first floor, which is plenty big enough and complicated enough to hide just about anything."

Maggie nodded. "Want to help me search?"

"Sure thing." Gideon set down his coffee and prepared to step into the next room.

But Maggie's warm little hand on his arm stopped him in his tracks. "What about Rex?" she asked when he met her eyes.

It was an excellent question. "He's a suspect as far as I'm concerned."

"Do you think we should tell the sheriff's office?"

Gideon wrestled with his response. "At this point, I don't think we stand to gain anything. If I was on this investigation, I'd be watching Rex Dunham very carefully, but I wouldn't want to bring him in for questions yet. I can already tell you his alibi—that he was at home sleeping in bed, and nobody would argue with that, even if he doesn't have a witness. But this new sheriff gal might try to call him in for questions. I don't want to risk that, not until we've had a chance to gather some solid evidence against him. The last thing we want to do is let him know that we're on to him."

"Why not?"

It was an innocent question, and Gideon smiled out of gratitude that Maggie was the innocent kind of person who didn't understand how criminals worked—would probably never understand how criminals worked, because she didn't have a criminal mind. But he knew enough about the criminal mind to answer with absolute certainty.

"There's a very good chance if he feels threatened he's going to escalate—that means he'll take more risks and use greater violence." His smile flattened as the gravity of the situation weighed on him. "We need to keep our heads down and not let on to what we suspect. It's the only way I can keep you safe."

NINE

Maggie was ready to tear the house apart looking for clues, but Gideon insisted they check the woods for footprints first. She couldn't really argue with that. He ran home to change clothes and she took a quick shower. By the time she pulled on her sneakers, Gideon was at the front door with donuts.

"After the morning we've had, we deserve a little chocolate-frosted pick-me-up," Gideon said, opening the lid on the small box so she could choose a donut.

"Mmm, you found my weakness," she chided him, though she wasn't about to turn down the delicious-looking treats. "And just when I was starting to lose weight from all this physical labor I've been doing."

Gideon gave her a long look over the box lid. "We can't let that happen," he said, closing the box after her and heading for the rear of the house.

With the donut half-raised to her lips, Maggie froze and watched him go. Had he meant that to sound like the semiflirtatious compliment she'd heard? Surely he wasn't advocating she keep the extra curves that clung to her five-foot-two-inch frame? Obviously she'd heard him wrong, or maybe he'd heard her wrong, or... Anyway, there was no way she could ask him about it, not without embarrassing herself. Instead she let the first bite of donut melt in her mouth as she headed out the back door after him.

Maggie followed Gideon as he picked up the trail of footprints where they headed into the woods, and managed to pick his way through the carpet of leaves that covered the ground. Autumn was already well under way, its crisp scent thicker in the woods, and that morning there was a decided chill in the air. Winter would be just around the corner.

Fortunately, the rapid scramble of Gideon and his prey had left enough muddied streaks that they were able to pick out something of the trail as they went. But the deeper into the woods they ventured, the fewer and farther between the prints became.

"I don't know," Gideon sighed, crouching to inspect a print as he polished off the last donut. "That looks like it came from my shoes. I think we're already past where I lost him."

Maggie crossed her arms over her chest to ward off the cold, wishing she'd opted for a warmer jacket, or maybe a coat. Still, she knew part of the chill she felt had nothing to do with the weather, and everything to do with the perp who'd gotten away. "I haven't seen any clear prints at all," she said with regret. "Nothing that could help us identify a suspect."

"We don't know where he went from here, but the highway that runs out of town is just on the other side of this hill. He may have had a car parked there."

"Let's check it out."

They tromped back through the woods until they found the highway. Matted grass indicated a spot where a car may have been parked at one time, but Gideon shook his head when Maggie asked if any of it could be traced back to a particular vehicle.

"The grass obscures the tread marks. There's not enough of a print to tell what size of tire drove through here, or when." He sighed. "We should get back to the house."

Gideon felt impatient about the time they'd wasted searching the woods, especially since they hadn't found anything. And the worst news was, Maggie wasn't safe at the house. He'd seen how close their intruder had come to getting past the armoire in the basement. A skinnier fellow could have slipped right through. He'd shoved the unit back against the door and double-barricaded the lock, but that didn't mean the perp wouldn't just find a different means of breaking in next time. It wouldn't take two seconds to shatter a window and step right in.

Fortunately, Gideon had an idea, though he doubted Maggie would readily agree to it. If she was spooked already, she might try to resort to going back to Kansas City. He couldn't stand the idea of that.

They stepped back into the dismantled kitchen and Maggie set to work running a fresh pot of coffee at the little cupboard unit that was all that remained of the kitchen they'd torn apart.

Knowing he had to be firm and forward with his idea before Maggie made up her mind to leave Holyoake, Gideon told her bluntly, "The intruder may return. I don't want you staying here alone."

"But I don't have anywhere else to go," she protested. "Besides, I think it's a good idea to have someone staying at the house around the clock. If anyone tries to break in again, we can catch them next time. If I'm not here, whoever it is might find whatever they're looking for, and then we'll never know who killed my father."

In spite of himself, Gideon found himself smiling at

Maggie's determination. He knew she was scared, but she was dead set on catching her father's killer and bringing him to justice, even if it meant putting herself in the path of danger. But he also knew he'd never forgive himself if anything happened to her. "I agree. The only reason the perp got away today was because it took me too long to get to him. The sound of my engine gave him too much warning—but if I'd have come on foot, he would have made it into the house and had a chance to hurt you. I can't risk letting that happen."

"So what do you think we should do?"

"We need to finish that southwest bedroom upstairs."

Maggie gave him a confused look.

"You're getting a couple of roommates."

"I am? Who?"

"I'll move in upstairs. That way I'll be on-site to apprehend the killer if he returns."

Maggie's mouth fell open.

"And I'm going to ask my niece to stay with you in your room downstairs."

"Your niece?" A pained look crossed Maggie's face. "You mean Kayla?"

Unsure what her distressed expression meant, Gideon explained, "Kayla is my brother Bruce's daughter. She just turned twenty-three and works as a nurse at the Holyoake hospital, but she still lives in her folks' house. She's having a hard time right now with her dad in prison and her family under investigation. I think she needs to get out of her father's house and get her head on straight. She's talked about moving out, but it's hard to find a place to rent in Holyoake these days."

Maggie nodded with understanding, but she still looked distraught as she poured them both mugs of coffee and led the way to the parlor. She settled into the opposite end of the sofa from him, and bent her leg up onto the seat as she turned to face him.

"You said Kayla's been having a tough time." Maggie held his gaze with a deep sorrow that her glasses did nothing to hide. "I've always wondered, ever since her illness when she was little…" Her voice dropped off and she looked to the ceiling as though she was looking for help. "Did she recover?"

Gideon felt Maggie's struggle as she tried to articulate her question. Once she finally got the words out, he felt relieved, and was glad to report, "As far as I know she came out of that just fine. She's bright and healthy." The smile that leaped to Maggie's face cheered him. "Kayla's just troubled, that's all. I think you'll understand once you meet her."

Maggie understood exactly what Gideon meant the moment Kayla stepped out of her car. The girl's darkly dyed hair hung over her thickly lined eyes, and her nearly black painted lips turned down in a frown. Resentment seemed to resonate from her, though her expression softened slightly when Maggie greeted her.

"Thanks for coming to stay with me," Maggie called out from the porch.

Kayla climbed the worn steps. "It's cool. I've always wanted to stay in a haunted house."

Maggie exchanged looks with Gideon, who appeared to be as surprised as she was at his niece's comment.

"It's not haunted," Gideon corrected Kayla.

"Ri-ight." Kayla rolled her eyes and walked past Maggie into the house. "It was a funeral home. And that creepy old lady used to live here. Where's my room?"

"You're sharing the first-floor bedroom with Maggie," Gideon explained, and proceeded to take charge of getting

Kayla settled in. As the young woman unpacked her things, Maggie and Gideon tiptoed off to the kitchen.

"Do you think she's okay about coming here?" Maggie asked.

"This is the perkiest I've seen her."

If Kayla's downhearted demeanor was relatively perky, Maggie didn't want to think about how the young woman must have behaved before her arrival. Though she was infinitely relieved to have discovered that the toddler who'd been so frightfully ill all those years ago had grown into a healthy adult, she wasn't about to stop praying for her now.

The next Saturday morning, as Maggie sat with her feet up on the old Victorian sofa sketching kitchen ideas, Gideon walked up beside the sofa and looked over her shoulder.

"I know what you're thinking," Maggie said after he'd stood there a full minute in silence. "The kitchen's still too small, isn't it?" Gideon had given her numbers on the cost of expanding the kitchen weeks before, but Maggie had balked at the high cost, doubtful they'd be able to recover their investment.

But Gideon didn't push for those plans. "Actually, I was thinking about how we might be able to expand the space without knocking out the back wall of the house."

"How?"

Gideon's hand swept past her head and touched a spot on her drawing. "We could knock out this wall here."

"But that's where the basement stairs are," Maggie protested.

"We can put a set of stairs under the front staircase. If we knock out that wall, we'd be giving ourselves nearly twice the space. Who knows, we might even decide to open the kitchen all the way through to the dining room. It would give the whole back half of the house a more open feel."

Maggie sat up straighter and spun around to face him.

"Knock out the whole stairway?" she clarified.

"It would vastly increase the size of the kitchen, but for minimal cost." Gideon smiled at her.

"Wouldn't we need to change the plans at the city office first?" They'd already been through the modification process on her father's original building permit when Maggie decided to make the home a single-family dwelling instead of apartments.

"It's not a load-bearing wall, so we don't need approval."

"You're the legal expert." She grinned. "Get your sledgehammer."

Gideon's smile grew. "You're serious?"

"Sure." She attributed the fluttering in her stomach to the nerves she felt at the idea of knocking out a wall. Surely it had nothing to do with the way Gideon smiled at her. "Just hurry up before I change my mind."

Gideon analyzed the wall he was planning to knock out. He knew he had to be sure to only disturb the portion of wall he intended to remove. They already had plenty parts of the house torn up. He didn't want to demolish anything more than he needed to.

"Measure twice, cut once," Maggie said as she observed him running around the sides of the enclosed basement stairs with his measuring tape.

"Your father always used to say that," Gideon informed her with a smile.

"I know."

Accustomed as he was to ignoring his feelings for Maggie, Gideon hardly had to work at stifling the warmth that flooded his heart as Maggie returned his smile. Instead he frowned at the wall and stepped halfway down the stairs, measuring again.

"Or measure three times," Maggie said with a giggle, but her expression grew serious when Gideon poked his head back into the kitchen from the stairs. "What's wrong?"

"Tell me I'm not imagining things." Gideon reviewed the measurements he'd taken, including the glaring discrepancy from the measurements on either side of the walls, and the much smaller space inside the stairwell.

"You're not imagining things," Maggie confirmed after she'd watched him measure each in turn again. "There's a hollow space inside the wall, isn't there?"

"It's more than just a space. It's practically its own room. But what is it there for? And why is it walled off?" Gideon questioned aloud.

"Suspicious," Maggie murmured, using the same word her father had used in his phone call to Gideon right before he'd died.

"Do you think so?" Gideon instinctively drew closer to Maggie and dropped his voice. "Do you think this hollow space might have been what your father was referring to? It's not in the basement, but it does involve the basement stairs."

"It makes sense." Maggie leaned toward him and dropped her voice, as well. "Dad always noticed things like that. And if he was working with plans for renovating the whole house, he'd have been taking measurements. All the plans I've found that he left behind had to do with the second floor, except for some very rough preliminary drawings. He hadn't done specifics on the first floor yet."

"That we know of," Gideon pointed out, wondering if perhaps Glen Arnold's killer had taken any such notes that would have revealed the existence of the hidden space. "Do you think we should still knock out the wall?"

"Definitely. We need to see what's back there."

Gideon agreed with Maggie's decision. Furthermore, he wanted to hurry up with the project, since Kayla would be ending her shift at the hospital early that afternoon, and he was hoping to spend time with her later in the day. Part of his reasoning for inviting his niece to stay at the house had been to get her to open up about what she knew of her father's activities. The girl had been largely silent on the issue, and Gideon was hopeful that she might know something that might help his case. And he was also worried about her.

"Stand back, then," Gideon instructed Maggie. "You might even want to open the back door. This will throw up a lot of dust and we could use the extra ventilation." He grabbed his sledgehammer from the organized collection of larger tools he'd lined up in the corner of the kitchen.

With a couple of preliminary taps, Gideon pulled back and drove the sledge home. The heavy head sank through the plaster into the lath, splintering wide cracks and sending large pieces raining down.

At the same instant, a chorus of screeching and screaming erupted inside the wall, and a brown cloud of bats flew through the new opening into the kitchen.

Maggie screamed as Gideon dropped the sledgehammer and covered her from the cloud of flying rodents. He felt their frightened bodies thumping into him, clawing their way past his head, no doubt blinded by the light of day. He wrapped his arms protectively around Maggie's thick hair, which, as usual, was hardly contained by her ponytail holder. If the bats got tangled in her hair, he'd have a mess on his hands trying to get them out.

Tucking her tightly against him, Gideon tried to cover Maggie as much as he could while the disoriented bats screamed and screeched through the kitchen. The light-blinded animals gradually began to find their way out the open back door—or into other areas of the house. Gideon couldn't even begin to estimate how many of them had been living in the hidden space in the wall.

As the frantic screeching died down, Gideon relaxed the hold he had on Maggie, but he didn't let her go. She clung to him, her little hands knotted around his shirt, her face buried in his shoulder.

He didn't want to let her go. She felt so right there, and she seemed to want him to hold her as much as he wanted to keep her in his arms. All the feelings he'd been trying for weeks to tamp down rose like a well inside his heart, and he struggled with what to do next.

He should probably let her go. The bats had stopped screeching. The moment had passed. If he held on to her any longer he'd really have some explaining to do.

Maggie clenched her hands tightly around the soft fabric of Gideon's worn work shirt. She could hear his heart thumping hard under her ear, and the musky scent of hard-working man teased her nose. His strong arms enfolded her, covering her from the onslaught of bats.

Obviously, he was just trying to protect her. That's what Gideon Bromley was all about—protecting the people of Holyoake County. Clearly the way he held her close meant nothing, at least not to him. She needed to remember that.

"Um, Gideon?"

"Yeah?" His arms loosened slightly around her.

"I think there's a bat in my hair."

Gideon shifted slightly, but didn't let go of her. "You're right. Hold still."

"Bats can carry rabies. I hope you're wearing gloves."

"I still have my leather work gloves on. But don't worry, I'm not going to let him bite either of us."

Maggie smiled. If anyone would have ever told her that she'd be happy to have a bat in her hair, she never would have believed them. But if it meant she got to stay close to Gideon for a few moments longer, she didn't mind the bat one bit. "Don't hurt it," she whispered as the critter gave a little cry.

"He's pretty tangled in there." Gideon struggled with the winged rodent a few moments longer, then sighed. "I think I'm going to need to cut him out."

"Don't hurt him!" Maggie shrieked again.

"Your *hair*," Gideon clarified, "I'm going to have to trim away a little of your hair. Unless you really don't want me to."

"Oh, no, that's fine," Maggie assured him. "Do you have anything to cut with?"

"Tin snips in my tool belt."

"Okay. That should probably work." Maggie wasn't sure if she still needed to stand pressed close to him as she was, but he hadn't made any move to push her farther away, and anyway, she was short enough that their current stance gave him a good view of the bat.

She decided to stay right where she was, holding on to his shirt for balance as she all but held her breath waiting for him to free the entangled creature. She felt Gideon's heartbeat thumping below her cheek, and wondered how long the bat's emancipation would take.

Finally, after a frightening amount of cutting and no shortage of pulling on her hair, Gideon took a step back and carried the traumatized creature out the back door, setting him on the brick patio, where he quickly shook himself free of the last of the hairs and took to the sky.

Maggie watched the critter fly away until he disappeared in the direction of the woods. She felt reluctant to face Gideon again after clinging to him for so long. As the bat's cries faded into the distance, Gideon tromped into the house ahead of her. Maggie stayed back, trying to sort out the tumultuous feelings that she couldn't deny any longer.

She'd always known Gideon was a good-looking fellow, in his own sharp-featured sort of way. He was strong and astute and comfortable just being silent—something she particularly enjoyed about him, since she'd never liked feeling pressured to make small talk. Obviously he was a competent worker and a man of integrity, who'd held up remarkably well in spite of the investigation against him. She had no end of respect for him.

And there had been moments when they'd been working together that she'd felt a connection to him, maybe even something more than simple attraction. But who was she kidding? She was frumpy, dorky Maggie Arnold. Never in a million years would Gideon Bromley be interested in her. She hadn't even considered it as a possibility.

It still wasn't a possibility. She hadn't forgotten the incident two decades before that had landed Kayla in the hospital. Even if the girl had recovered and grown into a healthy, if troubled, adult, that didn't mean the whole

Bromley family blamed her father any less for her illness. Though he hadn't said anything since she'd been back to indicate he held any lasting resentment for what had happened, she could still recall the conversation she'd heard him having with his brother, Bruce. They'd blamed her father for what had happened. Not even twenty years' time could change that.

Even if Gideon was willing to look past that event, it still wouldn't change the differences between them. The Bromley family was wealthy and had always been well respected in Holyoake. Maggie and her father had been shunned after everyone had become ill in her father's apartment house. Though no one who'd attended her father's funeral had spoken of that long-ago event, Maggie still felt the weight of it. She could still recall the words of judgment people had whispered.

No, Maggie and Gideon were from two completely different families. He was so many times more respected than she was. Her father had mentioned to her years before that Gideon had been elected by a large margin. Holyoake loved him—or they had before his brother's crimes. Holyoake had rejected her. No matter how she might feel about him, there was no chance Gideon would ever see her as anything more than a person who needed his help.

She was infinitely grateful for all the help he'd given her, not only toward fixing up the house, but in looking for her father's killer and keeping her safe. And he'd been volunteering all the time he'd spent working on the house. What kind of awful person would she be if she returned his kindness with an unwanted crush? He would be so disgusted with her if he knew how she felt about him.

Maggie took a deep breath of the cool autumn air before she stepped back into the kitchen. Whatever had just happened between them meant nothing. It couldn't possibly. The only thing that had changed was her resolve. She'd have to make every effort to hide the truth from Gideon. Absolutely, under no circumstances, could she let on for even a moment that she was falling in love with him.

TEN

Gideon peeled away the plaster and lath from the opening he'd made on the wall. Other than a disgusting heap of bat guano, there didn't seem to be anything in the hidden room—certainly not anything suspicious. He tried to rein in his disappointment.

"Find anything?" Maggie asked behind him.

How could he face her? Not only had they bashed in the wall without finding anything, but he'd held her in his arms—and given her a not-so-flattering haircut. Her gorgeous locks would need professional help. He kept his head in the hole. "Nothing yet," he answered without turning around.

To his relief, Maggie didn't come any closer, but said after a moment's silence, "I think I hear Kayla's car. She must be back from her shift at the hospital. I'll see how she's doing."

While Gideon pulled away more of the wall, the two women entered the kitchen talking. Maggie's cheerful voice made the drone of Kayla's voice sound even flatter.

"We found a secret room hidden behind the wall," Maggie explained.

"Yeah, we have one of those at my house, too."

Gideon pulled his head away from what he was working on and looked at Kayla just in time to see the young woman's thickly lined eyes go wide.

"You have a secret room hidden behind the wall at your house?" Gideon clarified. "Where?"

Kayla nodded, looking as though she'd been just as startled by her announcement as any of them. His niece took a step back and leaned against the remaining section of wall. "I'd forgotten all about that," she continued, shaking her head, displaying far more concern than Gideon had seen her express in some time. "My dad had a secret room. I saw him come out of it once years ago. He told me it was nothing, that I couldn't tell anyone, that I should forget I ever saw it. I was always so intimidated by him." She shook her head slowly. "I think I really *did* forget about it until right now."

"No one else knows about it?" Gideon clarified.

"Not that I know of." Kayla still looked shocked by the realization of what she knew. "Do you think—?" She looked back and forth from Maggie to Gideon as though looking for answers of some sort.

"I think," Gideon suggested cautiously, "you should let the sheriff see what's inside. And the DNE would probably like to be there, too."

Maggie could feel Gideon's tension as they worked at clearing out the hidden room in the old Victorian. Obviously he couldn't help but wonder what Kayla's discovery might mean for his case. Maggie wondered, too. Though she usually let him keep his thoughts to himself, this time the issue was too pressing for her to remain silent.

"She's been gone almost an hour," Maggie said softly once they had the little room mostly cleaned out of plaster and residual bat material, and Gideon stood washing his hands at the sink.

"It could take a while." He dried his hands and fumbled the towel, dropping it at his feet.

Maggie bent quickly and picked it up for him, handing it to him as he leaned after it a moment later. Her eyes met his. "Nervous?"

His chuckle said that he was. "I probably shouldn't be, but..." He gave a shrug.

"This should be good news for your case, don't you think?"

Gideon didn't try to escape from her questions. Instead he leaned against the wall. "I'd like to think so, but I've underestimated my brother all this time. He cooked all the books they've found so far so that all the evidence says I was involved with his case. But *somewhere* he had to keep his real records, wouldn't he? If no one knew about this hidden room..." His voice trailed off with a hint of hope.

"So this could be it?" Maggie couldn't suppress her smile. She wished Gideon would feel encouraged. "This could be the missing evidence that could free you."

He closed his eyes and tipped his head back against the wall, and Maggie could see the worry etched into his features. Every sharp angle, every fine line of his handsome face had become familiar to her over the past several weeks. As he stood there now with his eyes closed, it was as though he'd allowed himself to be vulnerable with her. His next words confirmed it.

Gideon's dark eyes opened slowly. "I just don't see how my brother could do such a thing. Not just making the drugs, but running his operation out of a secret room in his house—right under his daughter's nose. And then to ask her to forget all about it?"

"Do you think she really didn't remember seeing it until just now?"

"I believe it," Gideon said with certainty. "Especially if this was several years ago, when she was even younger. Witnesses suppress memories all the time, especially if they're young or scared. Kayla's father is such a domineering personality. I'd always hoped he'd be gentler with his own family, but apparently not."

Maggie felt Gideon's regret and his sorrow for what his young niece had gone through. "Poor Kayla," she whispered.

Gideon nodded at her words. "She didn't deserve this. She's just a sheep."

"A sheep?" Maggie repeated softly. It was the closest Gideon had ever come to expressing something spiritual. Maggie had often wondered where he stood in matters of faith, but he had always been silent on that topic, just as he was so often silent about all the other personal areas of his life.

He looked a little embarrassed that she'd caught him making such a statement, but rather than clam up about it, he explained. "Sheep and wolves. It's a law-enforcement analogy. Wolves are the bad guys, people like my brother, who are vicious and ruthless and only after their own interests. They don't care who they have to tear apart to get what they want.

"Kayla's a sheep. She's innocent, but unfortunately quite helpless on her own against the wolves in her life."

As Gideon explained his thoughts, Maggie felt her respect for him growing. He was a lawman, through and through. He felt so much responsibility for the sheep under his care.

"And what about you?" she asked quietly. "I know

you're not a wolf, but you don't strike me as a sheep, either."

His dark eyes met hers. "I'm a sheepdog. On the outside, I'm more like a wolf. I'm a fighter. But I wouldn't do anything to hurt the sheep."

Maggie swallowed back the affection she felt as he spoke. "Your job is to protect the sheep," she noted quietly.

"Used to be," Gideon observed, his jaw tightening.

A few weeks before, he would have walked away after a personal revelation like that one. But today he didn't.

And a few weeks before, Maggie never would have had the courage to open up with him about her faith. But she cared so deeply for this strong, wounded man. She cared about his soul, so she pushed past her natural shyness and offered, "The Bible talks a lot about sheep."

To her surprise, Gideon perked up at her words. "Where's that?" he asked.

She hadn't expected the question, and wasn't sure exactly of the answer. Wishing she had a more specific verse to give him, she said, "Well, Jesus talks a lot about being the Good Shepherd, about how the Good Shepherd lays down his life for the sheep. I think it's in the Gospel of John somewhere."

Gideon looked serious and seemed to make a mental note of her words. "Sheepdogs answer to the shepherd."

Maggie nodded, her eyes never once leaving his face. There wasn't any mention of sheepdogs in the Bible that she knew of, but she understood what he was getting at. Gideon was no sheep, no doubt about that. He was a sheepdog. But he needed the Good Shepherd just as much as the sheep did. "The Shepherd doesn't just care for the sheep. The Shepherd cares for the sheepdogs, too."

The darkness of his eyes seemed to lighten to a warm

deep chocolate. Maggie would have loved to stand there looking into their depths forever, but Gideon cleared his throat, and she recalled her earlier resolve. He couldn't know how she felt about him.

"I should probably…" she began, but couldn't think of what she needed to do.

To her relief, Gideon seemed to feel the same need to end the conversation. "I think I'll head upstairs for a while."

"Great," she chirped, and stepped out of his way. As she watched him head for the stairs she said a silent prayer that he'd find peace for his wounded soul.

Gideon fished out the Bible that was among the few personal belongings he'd brought with him for his stay at the house on Shady Oak Lane. He'd been reading it as he got the chance, starting in Genesis and on through Exodus, which had been interesting enough, though he hadn't found many answers to his questions there. Lately he'd been slogging through Leviticus, a cryptic book that seemed to speak more to a world from thousands of years ago than it spoke to his world now. Maggie's tip about the Gospel of John was a godsend.

Stretching out on his mattress on the floor, he searched the table of contents until he found what he was looking for, feeling even more gratitude that Maggie had pointed him in the right direction. The Gospel of John was much nearer the end of the Bible. He wouldn't have gotten there for a long time the way he'd been going at it.

Unlike his journey through Genesis and Exodus, which had been interesting enough, if less than helpful, in the Gospel of John the words seemed to leap off the page, speaking straight to his heart. He got as far as chapter three and the verses seemed to burn through to his soul.

For God so loved the world that He gave His one and only Son, that whoever believes in Him shall not perish but have eternal life. For God did not send His Son into the world to condemn the world, but to save the world through Him. Whoever believes in Him is not condemned…

Gideon fought to blink back the tears that rose to his eyes. He'd felt everyone's condemnation ever since his brother had named him as an accomplice. In the eyes of the people of Holyoake, and probably in the eyes of the investigators, he was a condemned man. But if he believed in Jesus, he could be saved from condemnation in the eyes of God.

He didn't deserve God's pardon. He knew he didn't deserve it. He'd missed so many clues that should have tipped him off to his brother's activities, trusted in all the wrong things, including trusting his brother when he should have known better. He didn't deserve the gift God offered. But at the same time, he wasn't about to pass it up.

His words came out as a hoarse whisper. "I believe."

Gideon read until his tear-weary eyes could read no more. The words filled him with hope, in spite of all the troubles they'd experienced at the house, and in spite of the unresolved investigation against him. As he came to the end of the book, Gideon realized Kayla was home again. He could hear her talking and laughing with Maggie downstairs.

Laughing? Gideon hadn't heard Kayla laugh in longer than he could remember, but now her giggles rose with Maggie's and echoed through the empty house.

Gideon tromped down the stairs to see what they were up to. As he entered the torn-out kitchen, he saw Maggie seated with her back to him, her thick hair cropped short, and Kayla seated opposite, a fluffy brush in her hand as she painted something powdery on Maggie's face.

"Uncle Gideon!" Kayla waved her brush at him. "You're just in time for Maggie's big reveal. Wait—don't look yet. I'm not quite done with her makeup."

"What did you do to her?" Gideon asked, imagining Maggie with eyes painted dark like Kayla's. And what had happened to all her long hair?

"I fixed the haircut you gave her, for one thing," Kayla said smartly. "We're giving her hair to Locks of Love."

"They make wigs for children with medical hair loss," Maggie added, without turning around.

"Sounds like a good charity for a pediatric nurse to support," Gideon said once he found his voice. He was itching to see Maggie's face, but at the same time, he felt nervous for what havoc his niece might have wreaked on the unsuspecting woman.

Kayla took a step back and grinned at her handiwork. "Maybe I should have become a cosmetologist after all." She sighed. "But I had to choose one or the other, and nursing doesn't make a very good hobby." She giggled. "Okay, Uncle Gideon. What do you think?"

Maggie stood and turned to face him, her expression a little sheepish, though Gideon hardly noticed that part.

She looked stunning. The cropped haircut curled cutely around her cheeks, and, well, he didn't know much about makeup, but, "Wow," he said, unable to fight back a smile.

Maggie grabbed her glasses and shoved them back onto her face.

Still wow, Gideon thought, be he tried not to look too excited. How had Maggie managed to hide her beauty all these years? And how was he supposed to work with her without acting on his growing affection?

Clearly the petite woman felt self-conscious about her new look. She blushed as she asked Kayla, "How many inches of hair do you think you cut off? We should measure it."

"Let me grab the measuring tape," Gideon volunteered, stepping back into the room where they were storing their small hand tools. He headed to the spot where the tools were kept in a neatly ordered line.

They weren't in a neat line anymore. Maggie wouldn't have left the tools in such disarray. She was an organized person—something he appreciated about her.

"Kayla, did you move my measuring tape?" he asked, hoping his niece had innocently borrowed it.

"I haven't touched any of your stuff," the young woman called to him from the other room.

Maggie appeared at his elbow in an instant. "It's gone?"

Though he would have liked to have been able to shield her from what had happened, it was already too late. She'd already seen the mess that had been made of their tools. "What else is missing?"

Gideon took a quick inventory. "Several small hand tools—all the things that are easy to carry." He shook his head. "I just used that measuring tape before we broke out the wall. We haven't left the house since then."

He met Maggie's eyes and saw the fear there. "Someone must have come into the house and stolen them while we were in the other room."

Though he hated to admit it, Maggie was right. They'd been so engrossed in cleaning out the hidden room, and then later he'd been absorbed with reading his Bible. Someone could have easily entered the house without their realizing it. But they could have walked in on them at any moment. Who would be foolish enough to take such a risk?

"Has the front door been unlocked while we've been home?" Maggie asked him.

"Yes," he admitted, already regretting leaving it that way. "I thought since we were both in here we'd be okay. Besides, with Kayla coming home from work I figured she'd appreciate not having to unlock the door."

Maggie nodded, and her eyes darted around the room to where the old furniture that came with the house still loomed like sheet-draped monsters in the corners. "Do you think…?" she started hesitantly.

"If someone came in while we were home…" He held her eyes as he picked up on what she was getting at.

"They might still be here," Maggie finished in a whisper.

Gideon nodded and stepped quietly past Maggie to look behind a large mirrored buffet that sat at odd angles with some other furniture in the corner. A person could hide in that space. It might be a tight fit, but he wasn't going to rule it out for that reason alone.

Wishing he had a sidearm on him, Gideon did a quick sweep of the room while Maggie got down on the floor to look underneath anything that had decent space under it. After pounding up the stairs and checking there, Gideon came back down, shaking his head.

"Do you think we should report this?" Maggie asked quietly.

Entering the room from which the tools had been taken, Gideon looked back at the dusty surface where the tools had been lying. The dust had hardly been disturbed. Once again, there would be no fingerprints to help them ID a suspect. "There's not much a sheriff can do now," he said, sighing.

"Uncle Gideon?" Kayla sounded breathless as she entered the room behind them. "Did you realize it's been snowing all morning?"

"Yes." On top of everything else, winter was catching up to them. But what did that have to do with anything?

"If you hurry," Kayla continued, "you might be able to follow the footprints before they get completely covered by snow."

"Footprints?" Gideon wheeled around excitedly.

"In the backyard." Kayla nodded. "They look like they head off toward the woods."

"Let me grab my coat," Maggie said. She returned from the hall closet seconds later and tossed Gideon his heavy jacket before throwing her coat over her shoulders on her way to the back door.

Gideon hurried after her and was relieved to see shoe-shaped indentations running from the side of the house through the snow toward the woods. The swirling flakes had already begun to obscure the marks. "Thanks, Kayla," Gideon called as he checked where the footprints had originated. He couldn't be certain how old they were, but neither he nor Maggie nor Kayla had been in the backyard that day—certainly not anywhere near the woods.

"They came out through the front door," Gideon observed aloud as he and Maggie backtracked their route, then headed off in the direction they led toward the wooded hills.

Maggie hurried after him as they followed the even strides. "These prints don't look big enough to belong to Rex Dunham," she noted. "They actually look pretty close to the size of the tracks we found by the shed the day you saw someone back here. That was when Bernie Gills' Taser was stolen, wasn't it?"

"It sure was." With years of investigative training and practice behind him, Gideon had already made the connection on the footprint size, but he still didn't know what to make of it. "The only way we're going to find who made these tracks is to follow where they lead."

They made their way through the woods, where the trees had disrupted the pattern of snowfall. In some places the footprints were easier to see. In other places, they disappeared completely. "This is a different path than the one I followed the other night," Gideon told Maggie.

"I know." She smiled back at him, her red lips lovely in contrast to the white snow. "But that would make sense if we're following a different person."

Her smile lightened Gideon's heart in spite of the tension he felt, and as Maggie stumbled a step closer to him through the uneven woods, he instinctively reached out and took her hand. Her gloveless fingers felt cold.

"Do you think they're working together?" Maggie asked, meeting his eyes.

It took Gideon a moment to recall who they were talking about. Maggie's cute haircut was too distracting. "The suspects," he said blankly, for lack of a more coherent response.

"Mmm-hmm." Maggie looked up at him, her pretty face full of trust.

Gideon looked down at the footprints they were following. He had to get his head on straight, but the touch of Maggie's cold fingers sent a distracting shiver up his arm, and with the makeover Kayla had given her, all Gideon really wanted to do was stand there holding Maggie's hand and looking at her. But he couldn't do that.

Forcing himself to recall what Maggie had asked him—something about their suspects working together—Gideon finally worked out a response. "Could be," he said noncommittally, tugging her along in the direction the footprints led. "But we won't know for sure until we find out who they are."

The prints seemed to dart along a path as they followed the place where the edge of town met the Loess Hills. For several hundred yards, the fading footprints simply followed a path. But then, as the path bent back toward town, the footprints headed inexplicably deeper into the woods.

Crouching to inspect the trail that was becoming more difficult to see as the rate of snowfall picked up, Gideon narrowed his eyes. "They head deeper into the hills," he observed.

"I think so," Maggie murmured in agreement. "But we need to hurry. It's hard to see anything of these prints anymore."

"We can't hurry too much or we'll miss where they lead."

"I know." Maggie trotted after him as they increased their pace. "But the snow is really starting to come down."

Gideon felt the same sense of desperation filling him that he'd felt as they'd traced the footprints through the woods the morning he'd chased off their perp. Different-size footprints, different direction, but in both cases, their trail had disappeared, leaving them looking around, grasping at nothing, all but lost in the woods themselves.

They slowed their pace, and finally Gideon stopped. "See anything?"

Maggie bit her lip and shook her head.

"We lost them again."

But Maggie was squinting off into the distance. "Maybe not. What's that over there?"

ELEVEN

Maggie hurried over to the strange formation of sticks that seemed to form an odd shelter in the woods. "Do you think it's just some kids' fort?" she asked as they neared the precarious dwelling, a skeleton structure of limbs that formed a tepee with space just big enough for the two of them to crouch inside.

"Could be. But what's this?" Gideon ducked into the ramshackle stick-built hut and pointed to an array of familiar objects.

"Those are the items that were stolen from the Dumpster." Maggie knelt down for a closer look. "What do you suppose…?" She began to reach for one of the old glass bottles she recognized as being one she'd bagged up and tossed out, but Gideon's strong hand closed gently over her fingers.

"Better not touch. There could be fingerprints."

Maggie straightened and backed her way out of the little fort. "Do you really think this could be related to our suspect? It looks like a child's hand-built fort. They've just decorated it with items found in our Dumpster."

"I don't know." Gideon's eyes were fixed on the arrangements of bottles and vacuum attachments and other odd containers. "Those footprints looked too big for a child."

"True. They were certainly a lot bigger than my feet. I wear a size six shoe—those had to have been a woman's nine or ten, at least. Maybe they belonged to an adolescent boy."

Gideon took another step back from the fort and looked around them through the swirling snow to the deep woods that clung to the hillside. "We've come over a mile from the house, I'd say. And this fort is a good ways from town. Who lets their kids run in that wide of a circle?"

"If it was an older kid," Maggie mused.

"But do older kids play like this?" Gideon looked at the awkward fort and the eccentric collection of objects salvaged from their trash. "And what about the message written in the Dumpster?"

Maggie understood what he was getting at. "It does seem strange." Strange, but not suspicious. Too many things still didn't fit. "Do you see any sign of Bernie's Taser? Or the tools that were taken this morning?"

"No." Gideon surveyed the hillsides, and Maggie looked over the area with him. All trace of the footprints had faded under the heavy snow. The former sheriff looked lost in the sea of white, and the confusion in his eyes only reinforced his bewildered appearance. He threw up his hands in disgust, his expression distraught. "What do I know?" he asked aloud, as much to the snow and the woods as to her.

Maggie wanted to comfort him, but she didn't know how. She felt the same sense of confusion that showed so clearly on the former sheriff's face. They'd hit so many dead ends. And what they'd found this time only made the case that much more bizarre.

"I used to trust my training, my instincts," Gideon

continued. "I used to think I was a good sheriff. But Bruce—" His voice caught on his brother's name, and he kicked at the ground, leaving a dark slash of dirt in the white snow.

Placing a tentative hand on his arm, Maggie looked up at him, wishing she knew what to say to bring him some peace. "What your brother did wasn't right. He took unfair advantage of you. That doesn't make you a bad sheriff."

"I should have figured it out. I should have caught him." His dark eyes burned through the swirling white. "Now I don't even know what's happening at your house. Too many things don't add up."

Maggie felt his sorrow squeezing her heart. "God knows," she whispered quietly.

Slowly the tension eased from Gideon's face. "He does," the hardened man agreed softly. "Do you think He'll ever reveal it all to us?"

"I don't know. The best thing we can do right now is trust Him."

Gideon clasped one warm hand over where Maggie still clutched his arm with her fingers. "Trust Him," he repeated, "and try to find our way back to the house before this blizzard gets any worse."

At that, Maggie realized just how thickly the snow had begun to fall. They'd have a challenge finding their way back. "We should probably hurry."

They trudged back the way they'd come, blinking back the white flakes that stuck to their eyelids and matted in their hair. Maggie's mind swirled like so much falling snow as the issues surrounding them tugged at her heart. What had Gideon's comments meant? She knew he blamed himself for not catching his brother, but he'd shown a new sense of peace the moment she'd mentioned God.

What did that mean? Where did Gideon stand with God? Though she usually felt far too self-conscious to make such a bold invitation, the burning in her heart was too much for her to ignore. "Gideon?" she asked as they slogged through the snowy woods.

"Hmm?"

"I was thinking about inviting Kayla to come to church with me tomorrow. Do you think she'd go for something like that? I feel like she's started to open up to me, but I don't want to chase her away."

For a long time, they plodded on in silence, until Maggie began to wonder if Gideon was going to answer her question. But he must have been weighing her suggestion, because finally he said, "Why don't we both ask her to come with us?"

In her surprise, Maggie stumbled, and Gideon reached out and caught her arm.

"If that's okay?" he clarified. "I don't want to intrude."

"You mean you want to come to church with me?" she asked breathlessly. She quickly added, "And Kayla?"

"Yeah."

Maggie couldn't stop herself from beaming up at him. "I think that would be the best possible thing." Then she realized how her words must sound. "For Kayla." She clarified.

"I think it will be good for Kayla," Gideon said, trudging on in the direction of the house, his hand still keeping a steady hold on her arm. "I think you've been a good influence on her already."

"She's a good kid," Maggie murmured agreeably, but inside her, she felt her heart thumping guiltily. Had she been good for Kayla? Or was she just trying to make up for the ordeal the girl had gone through years before while living as a toddler in her father's rental house?

When they reached the house, Maggie looked with fondness at the sprawling dwelling that had caused them so much trouble, and she felt a grin spread across her face. In spite of all that had happened there, she'd come to care about the house and what happened to it. Already she could see improvements she and Gideon had made together.

Then she noticed her car parked along the street in front of the house, and sighed. "I suppose I'll have to move my car so the snowplows can get past."

"Unless you want it buried," Gideon agreed. "Would you like me to move it for you?"

"That would be sweet of you. Let me get you my keys. They're right inside on the—"

She froze and looked up at Gideon.

He seemed to have realized it at the exact same moment she did.

"Next to the small hand tools?" he asked.

They both rushed inside to the spot where the tools had been taken. Maggie could see a faint scratching outline in the dust where she'd been keeping her keys.

"You're sure you didn't put them somewhere else this time?" Gideon asked, a hint of hope in his voice.

"No." Maggie wished she could tell him otherwise. "Not only have I been making it a point to put them in the same place, but I distinctly remember putting them down right here after I came back from the grocery store this morning."

"So our perp has your keys." Gideon seemed to snap into lawman mode. "Including your car keys, the key to this house, the garage." He looked at her to fill in the gaps.

"And the truck I inherited from my father. That's about it. All my Kansas City keys are on another ring in my bedroom, along with the spare to my car, so at least I can still move it for the snowplows."

"We'll need to change the locks on the house right away," Gideon insisted.

Maggie felt horrible. "And the garage," she agreed.

"Were there any other keys on the key ring?"

In her mind, Maggie could picture the simple ring of keys. "Car, truck, house, garage and then there was a brass key. I have no idea what it was to, but it had fancy scrollwork all up the side. I found it in the glove box of my father's truck and kept it on the ring in case I ever found what it went to. It didn't fit anything in his old apartment." Afraid she was babbling, Maggie looked up to see Gideon looking at her intently.

"In your father's truck?" Gideon asked, his voice a little breathless.

"Yes. Why is that significant?"

Gideon's face knotted as he appeared to wrestle with what to say.

"Do you think the key is important?" Maggie pressed.

"I don't know." He shook his head. "Do you remember when I told you about the call I received from your father the morning of his death?"

"Yes." Maggie felt her heart beat faster at the mere mention of that day.

"He called me from his cell phone and said he was here at the house. When I arrived twenty minutes later, he was dead. I don't believe he went anywhere in that time, and yet, during part of our conversation, I heard a dinging sound in the background, like the tone a vehicle makes when you've left the keys in the ignition. Later, when we searched the scene, we found the keys to your father's truck in the ignition."

Maggie tried to follow what Gideon was getting at. Sure, it wasn't a particularly good idea to leave keys in a vehicle, but in Holyoake, people did it all the time—especially in old work trucks like her father's, which weren't worth stealing anyway. "So you think he may have been in the truck when he called?" she asked.

"I've always wondered about that. It was only for a moment or two—not so much that he got in, but just opened the door and leaned in, or something."

"Leaned in to put something in the glove box?" Maggie felt her eyes widen, and when Gideon took a step closer to her, she didn't hesitate to reach for his arm. "Something suspicious, maybe? But why would he put it in the truck if he was planning to show it to you?"

Gideon let out a long breath. "I don't know. Maybe he suspected someone was watching him. Perhaps he'd seen his murderer approaching."

Maggie swallowed.

"We don't know what happened that morning." Gideon shook his head. "I just can't help thinking that if you've had the key this whole time, and if it may have come from this house…"

"'Give it back,'" Maggie quoted the words that had been scrawled in the Dumpster.

"Whatever it was they wanted, they have the key to the house now, so we'll have to change the locks immediately."

"The hardware store closed at five," Maggie noted. Dusk had fallen even as they'd returned from their trek through the woods.

"Then we'll have to drive to Omaha."

"In a blizzard? That's a three-hour round-trip in good weather. Can't we just park some furniture in front of the doors?"

Gideon's face displayed his concern, but he finally relented. "I don't suppose our perp is going to come back in a blizzard, anyway." He sighed. "I just hope this weather doesn't keep us from getting to church tomorrow."

"I'll pray that it doesn't."

Gideon was grateful to have Maggie sitting beside him through the worship service, helping him follow what was going on. He felt so out of place, not only because he didn't know anything about when to sit or when to stand or when to recite the prayers he didn't know the words to, but also because he felt the eyes of the people on him, watching him, no doubt wondering what the accused sheriff was doing in their place of worship.

But when Maggie smiled up at him, he realized he didn't care what anyone else thought. Maggie seemed to trust him. And what was it the Bible had said? God did not condemn those who believed in Jesus. So what if the rest of Holyoake thought he was guilty? God knew he was innocent, and that was all that mattered.

As the peace of that conviction settled over him, Gideon looked gratefully over at his niece. Kayla had eschewed her usual thick eye makeup in favor of a more natural look that morning, and it suited her. She began to look more like the Kayla he used to know.

But Maggie, on the other hand, looked ghostly pale. Gideon worried about her. She'd assured him she wasn't embarrassed to be seen with him, accused though he was, and he believed she was speaking the truth. But just as surely, something was on her mind. He wished he knew what it was.

He'd offered to drive to Omaha for a new lock set since the Holyoake hardware store was closed on Sundays, but they'd barely made it to church through the still-falling snow. Maggie had insisted the lock set could wait until Monday. So he knew that wasn't what was bothering her.

After the service they headed back to the house, where Maggie had left a roast and vegetables in a Crock-Pot for their lunch. She raised the lid and a savory aroma rose with the steam that escaped.

"Smells wonderful." Gideon watched her face carefully, hoping his words would bring a smile to her face.

But her eyes still looked haunted. "I'd give it another hour or so for the meat to get tender." She set the lid back in place and turned to face him.

Gideon didn't move from where he stood directly behind her, though she looked up at him as though she expected him to step aside so she could get by. "What's bothering you?" he asked quietly, aware that Kayla was in the other room, and reluctant to let her overhear their conversation.

"Me?" Maggie squeaked as though she was going to deny anything was wrong.

"Is it your stolen keys? The hidden room? Everything together?" Gideon wanted to place a comforting hand upon her shoulder, but the way she looked at him, he was afraid even that small gesture might send her running. "Have I done something to upset you?"

Her clear blue eyes looked up at him, and her mouth fell open just slightly. Gideon felt the urge to kiss her, but he held back those feelings. He had no right to get that close to her, but at the same time, he had to know what was bothering her. She meant too much to him, he couldn't let her obvious distress go unaddressed.

"You have been a blessing." Maggie shook her head and looked down. "I don't know what I'd do without your help."

Her newly cropped hair fell across her cheek, and Gideon reached out and gently pushed it back, in the same motion tilting her face back up so he could see her eyes. "Then what is it? Something's bothering you."

"Everything." Anguish crossed her features. "And having Kayla here—"

"I thought the two of you were getting along well?"

"We are," Maggie rushed to assure him. "She's a great girl. It's just that every time I see her, I remember what happened." Her voice faded.

"What happened?"

"When she was a little girl." Maggie shook her head sorrowfully. "Living in my father's house. We'd had several reports of strange odors, but no one ever found the source. Then she got sick and almost died." Maggie covered her face with her hands. "I wish I could go back in time and undo all that. I wish it had never happened. I feel so responsible."

"Whoa." Gideon brushed her hand away so he could see her eyes again. "Maggie, are you talking about what happened twenty years ago when we were in high school?"

"Yes."

"I don't blame you or your father for that."

But Maggie insisted, "Gideon, I heard you. I overheard you talking with your brother in the hallway at the hospital when I went to give Kayla a get-well balloon. Bruce said it was all my family's fault, that we rented out a health hazard, that my father was to blame. You were so mad, both you and Bruce were so mad—at my dad, at both of us."

"No." Gideon sighed and pulled Maggie into his chest, wondering how she could have believed that all those years without saying anything. "I was mad. I was mad at your dad that day. I was so upset I confronted him. He insisted he hadn't done anything wrong, that he never made shoddy repairs on his houses. He told me if I didn't believe him, I could come to work for him and I'd see that he kept all his rentals in better shape than the code allowed. That's how I started working for him. He was right. He was a good man and an excellent landlord. I have no lack of respect for him."

Maggie's mouth fell open a little more as she looked up at him. Gideon wanted so much to kiss those lips. Instead he looked away and saw Kayla standing behind them.

"Sorry to interrupt," his niece said hesitantly. "I couldn't help but overhear."

"It's okay." Maggie shoved back a tear. "Maybe I should have said something sooner. But I felt so guilty. Everyone in town blamed my father for what happened to you."

Kayla nodded. "I was a little girl then, not quite three, but I still remember people talking about it. My father wanted everyone to believe my illness was your dad's fault. He spread those rumors. I—" She looked down and wrung her hands before looking up again. "I haven't let myself think about my dad ever since he was arrested. I was so mad at him. But ever since I remembered the secret room yesterday, I realized there might be other memories I've forgotten about that could help the investigators sort out what happened."

Gideon listened intently, so focused on what his niece was saying he hardly realized he still had his arm around Maggie's shoulders. Now he held her tight against him as he listened.

"I don't know how long my father was involved with making drugs," Kayla continued, "but I saw some of the books the investigators took out of that room yesterday. I saw the dates, the records. I think my father may have used drug money to found his transportation company. More than that, I think he may have founded his transportation company as a way of distributing the drugs he was making. He'd been making drugs since I was a little girl."

Kayla looked at Maggie with regret in her eyes. "The more I think about it, the more I become convinced that my own father made me sick that day. If he was cooking up a batch of meth in the house, the fumes would have created the exact symptoms everyone experienced—including the ones that almost killed me."

Maggie reached for Kayla, who stepped into a big hug from both of them. Gideon held them both, but the peace he'd felt at church that morning had already begun to disappear. Kayla's revelation only made him feel worse.

If his brother, Bruce, really had been running drugs all those years, how could Gideon have missed catching him for so long? Granted, Bruce was smooth and had clearly worked to gain his trust, while at the same time going to extreme lengths to cover his tracks. But that didn't change the simple fact that Gideon should have caught him long ago.

Instead, he'd failed. He'd failed Kayla, failed Maggie, failed Glen Arnold and failed all of Holyoake County. Who had he been fooling? He wasn't cut out to be sheriff. So it really made very little difference that he hadn't been directly involved with his brother's drug ring. He'd let Bruce get away with running drugs all those years. That, more than anything else, made him a guilty man.

While Maggie and Kayla hugged and shared repeated apologies for all the misunderstandings that had passed between their families, Gideon took a step back and headed up to his room. Maggie didn't need a failure like him in her life. And Holyoake County didn't need a failure for sheriff, either.

Maggie felt such tremendous relief after Kayla's revelation that she sailed through the rest of the afternoon, stripping old paint from the woodwork in the front parlor and marveling at the beauty of the wood underneath.

She felt like that wood—as if she'd been hiding under a heavy, choking coat of guilt all those years. With Kayla's words, the guilt had been stripped away. It was a freeing feeling.

Kayla helped out, chattering about all sorts of things now that they'd cleared the air between them. Maggie was so lost in her own thoughts, she didn't catch every word of what Kayla was saying until the girl stood back from the project and asked, "Well, why don't you?"

It took Maggie a second to recall what Kayla had been talking about. Something about her work as a nurse at the hospital, and how they were always so short staffed. "Work at the Holyoake Hospital?" Maggie asked incredulously once she caught back up to the conversation.

"Sure. You're a nurse. We don't have anybody who specializes in pediatrics. You'd be perfect."

"I couldn't possibly," Maggie protested quickly. She needed to squash Kayla's idea before the young woman became too attached to the crazy plan. "I live in Kansas City. I *belong* in Kansas City. I own a house there, and that's where my job is."

"But you own this house, don't you? And you could get a job in Holyoake." Obviously, Kayla didn't understand the complexity of the issues involved.

Maggie stood back and surveyed the progress they were making on the woodwork. She tried to collect her thoughts, but they were a jumbled mess. The whole idea that she might ever live in Holyoake again was simply absurd. She'd spent her teenage years wanting nothing more than to escape the town, and had immediately left for Kansas City after graduation, getting her nursing degree and her job at the hospital, and building a life for herself there. She'd spent the past sixteen years running away from Holyoake. Why would she ever return?

But how could she explain all that to Kayla in a way the young woman would understand? "My father died in this house," she said finally. "I don't think I could ever live here."

"Oh." Kayla's eyes fell, and she went back to her work. "Sorry if I reminded you of something painful."

"No, it's okay," Maggie assured her, but her heart stayed stuck on that point. She had too many painful memories in the house—memories of her father's death, and of the disturbing incidents that had taken place since then.

And if that wasn't reason enough, she had memories of Gideon in that house.

As she climbed into bed that night, Maggie found herself still sorting through her feelings. If she was brutally honest, she knew she'd developed feelings for the former sheriff—strong feelings like she'd never felt before.

But who was she kidding? He'd held her in his embrace that afternoon while Kayla had shared the truth of her father's history, and then he'd dropped his arms and walked away as though he couldn't put enough distance between them. She'd hardly seen him since.

Gideon was a wonderful man who'd so generously volunteered his time to help her with the house. Now more than ever, she realized he was simply trying to make up for her father's death. He felt guilty because he'd never caught her father's killer. She prayed he'd eventually realize that her father's death wasn't his fault.

The memory of the embrace they shared earlier filled her with a feeling of warmth, and she pulled the covers tight around her to ward off the incessant cold that filled the old house. For a few minutes, she let herself remember what it had felt like to be in Gideon's strong arms. She'd felt so protected, so safe, so warm.

A tear slipped onto her pillow. She hadn't been kidding when she'd told Kayla she needed to get back to Kansas City. Maybe she shouldn't even wait until the house was finished. Maybe she should go now—before she became too attached to Gideon. Before she let her heart get broken.

Sniffling back the tears, Maggie struggled to form a plan for leaving. She'd have to finalize some of the house plans since she couldn't make every decision from a distance. But she knew she could trust Gideon to make good decisions. She'd already learned they had similar tastes, and he knew what her feelings were about staying under budget. The thoughts rumbled through her tired mind.

Somewhere along the line she must have fallen asleep, because it felt much later when she awoke with a start at the sound of a loud noise echoing through the house.

Thump!

It only took Maggie's sleepy mind a second to realize what was going on. Their perp was back, trying to break into the basement again. But this time, she heard the telltale creak of Gideon's door on the second floor, and the nearly silent footfall as he made his way down the stairs in the darkness. He was going to catch her father's killer!

Maggie scrambled out of bed and threw on some clothes, trying not to wake Kayla, whose gentle snores from the other bed told her she hadn't heard a thing yet.

Shoving her glasses on her nose and grabbing a flashlight, she slipped on her shoes and leaped for the bedroom door just as Gideon's yell rent the night.

TWELVE

"Freeze!" Gideon's voice cut through the silent darkness, and Maggie could hear him swallow back the word *sheriff.* "Hold it right there!"

Maggie leaped out the back door just in time to see Gideon pulling a much bigger man up the cellar stairs. She trained her flashlight on the man's face.

It wasn't Rex Dunham.

"I'm not hurting anything," the man defended. "This is my mother's house."

Gideon looked at Maggie.

Maggie looked back at the perp, who blinked against the bright beam of the flashlight she had trained on him. "Danny?" she asked incredulously, taking in how much the once-little boy had grown. "Little Danny Creel?"

"Yes." He looked as though he was trying to see past the light she shined in his face. "Although I prefer *Dan* these days."

She lowered the beam. "Your mother doesn't live here anymore. The bank foreclosed on her over a year ago. I own this house now."

Surprise showed on the younger man's face. Maggie had known him years before and had even babysat for him a few times when she'd been in high school. She could hardly believe how much he'd grown, but then his mother had been a large woman, too, so he had it in his genes.

"I—I'm sorry." Dan Creel looked back and forth between Maggie and Gideon, a sincere apology written on his face. "I didn't realize. I guess I just assumed." His voice faded, and he appeared to be slowly absorbing the revelation. "It hadn't occurred to me that she might have moved."

"You don't talk to your mother much?" Gideon clarified.

Dan shrugged his massive shoulders. "I guess it has been a while. I wish she would have told me if she was having trouble making her house payments. I would have helped her out. But she was always so secretive."

The cold night air seeped through the thin clothes Maggie had thrown on in her haste, and she shivered. Immediately Gideon looked over at her and suggested, "Why don't we all go inside?"

"I'm sorry about the cellar door," Dan apologized as he followed them into the house. "You can send me a bill for the repair."

Gideon didn't acknowledge the offer, but seemed determined to extract some answers from the former owner's son. "Why were you trying to break into your mother's house, anyway?"

If possible, their would-be intruder looked even more sheepish. "She took something from me a long time ago. I wanted to get it back."

Maggie exchanged looks with Gideon before asking Dan, "You haven't been leaving notes around asking for it back, have you?"

Dan looked even more confused. "No, I'm sorry. I've tried to break into the basement a few times, but that's all."

But Gideon didn't look as though he bought the man's story. "I chased you through the woods last time, didn't I? Why didn't you explain yourself then?"

"You surprised me and I ran." Dan looked repentant, even embarrassed. "I figured I'd come back for what I wanted another time."

"Couldn't you just ask her for it?" Gideon's stern face said he wasn't buying the young man's excuse.

"I've tried that. Many times. My mother isn't the world's most reasonable person, if you've ever tried to talk to her."

"What's so important that you'd risk a breaking-and-entering charge to get it?" Gideon continued his interrogation, and Maggie stood back, watching him, glad she'd never had to face him when he was determined to get answers. The man was intimidating, staring down the much larger man without flinching.

Dan, on the other hand, looked remorseful. "I'm sorry. If I'd had any idea this wasn't my mother's house—"

"So breaking into your mother's house is okay?"

"Do you know my mother?"

"I've met her." Gideon crossed his arms across his chest, his expression challenging.

"Do you know how unreasonable she can be?"

"Just because a person's unreasonable, that doesn't give you a right to break into their home."

Maggie felt like a fly on the wall as she watched Gideon grill his suspect. To Dan's credit, he was apologetic, but didn't wither under Gideon's unrelenting onslaught of questions. As Gideon pressed him for specific answers, Dan gave specific alibis to explain that he couldn't have been responsible for any of the other incidents at the house. He didn't seem to know anything about the missing tools or the little hut in the woods, either, and looked sincere.

Finally, Gideon got around to asking the question Maggie's heart burned to hear.

"Where were you in the early morning hours of Saturday, September fourth?"

"Labor Day weekend?" Danny clarified.

Gideon nodded, his obsidian eyes unflinching.

"California. I was on the news. Live. I can get footage if you need it. I'm a private investigator. My partner and I had just unraveled a major missing person's case. All the major stations carried the story. You may have even seen it."

Maggie doubted that Gideon had even had enough time to glance at a television screen that weekend, between discovering her father's body and dealing with the unraveling drug case his brother had been behind.

"Get me that footage," Gideon said, a satisfied look crossing his face. He took a step back from the man and finally uncrossed his arms from over his chest.

Dan looked back between Gideon and Maggie again. "You're—you're not going to press charges?"

Gideon looked at Maggie.

She shrugged. "If he's going to pay for the damages to the door—"

"Yes. I can write you a check tonight," Dan offered.

"We'll need all your contact information. We may need to get in touch with you again." Gideon looked as if he was about to let the man go, but then he scowled again. "You never did say what your mother took from you that you were trying to get back."

The young man had begun to rise to standing, but now sat back down. "A pocket watch. She gave it to me when I was little, but then took it away again and hid it—I think in one of her hiding places in the basement."

"Why is this watch so important?"

"My father's name is inscribed somewhere inside that watch. When my mom saw me trying to take the watch apart, she was afraid I'd learn who my father was. She never wanted me to know his identity, so she took the watch away. I've tried asking her for it for years. A few months ago I asked again, and she said something about having hidden it in the wall." Dan's face knit into an uncertain expression. "I'm not sure exactly what she meant. She doesn't always make sense. But that's why I've been stopping here whenever I've been in the area. I hoped to find it."

Maggie felt sorry for the young man. He'd been an awkward kid with an intimidating mother, but she knew from babysitting him years before that he was gentle-natured, in spite of his daunting size. She wished she could do something to help him learn the identity of his father. "We'll keep our eyes out for that pocket watch," she offered. "We'll give you a call if we find anything."

Dan's eyes immediately brightened. "I'd appreciate that very much." He jotted down his contact information for Gideon, and thanked them again before he left.

"I'm so sorry for scaring you guys, and for breaking the door. Let me know if there's anything else I can do to make it up to you."

"I just hope we can find that watch for you," Maggie said as she waved goodbye. The young man crunched away through the snow, and Gideon pulled the door shut against the cold.

Already the pink light of dawn had begun to rise in the east.

Maggie stifled a yawn. "Another long day," she said, thinking of the sleep she'd lost and all the projects they had on their to-do list for the day.

"And another lead, gone."

"That pretty well clears Rex Dunham of any implication, doesn't it?" Maggie asked.

Gideon nodded. "The only reason we suspected him was because of the large size of the man I chased, but obviously I was chasing Dan, not Rex."

"But if Dan didn't kill my father, then who did?" Maggie asked as she started a pot of coffee, tossing in extra grounds. She could use the caffeine. They both could.

"The killer seems to have vanished. What clues do we even have left to go on?"

"Just my father's comment about finding something suspicious in the basement—and of course, all the little things that have been disappearing while we've been working on the house."

Suddenly Gideon spun around and grabbed Maggie by the shoulders, startling her.

"Hidden in the wall," he repeated, using the same words Dan had spoken in reference to what Lorna Creel had done with his pocket watch.

Maggie looked at the gaping hole in the kitchen wall that they'd scoured two days before. They hadn't found anything hidden in that wall.

Gideon gave her shoulders a gentle shake, and she met his eyes again.

"In the basement."

They both looked to the basement door as though whatever was hidden there might spring out at them in the next instant. But the door stayed innocently closed.

"I need a tape measure, crowbar, maybe a screwdriver."

"Ours were all stolen," Maggie reminded him.

"Stupid crook." Gideon made a face and dropped her shoulders. "I'm going to run to the hardware store now that it's finally open and the roads are clear. I'll be right back. Whatever you do—" he looked at the door to the basement, then back at her "—don't go into the basement until I get back."

Gideon made good time on his trip to the Holyoake Hardware Store, which fortunately opened early. As he arrived back at the house on Shady Oak Lane, he noticed Kayla's car was gone, and recalled her saying she had to work the early shift that morning. He climbed the front steps and was relieved to find Maggie, safe and sound, waiting for him in the front hall. She handed him a cup of coffee in his favorite mug.

"Thanks." He swapped his bag of purchases for the drink.

Maggie pulled the new tape measure from the bag. "So you think there's a hidden room in the basement, too."

Swallowing a swig of coffee prepared just the way he liked it, Gideon explained, "There may well be a correlating space just below the one we found. I suspect those stairs used to be a lot bigger than the cramped set that leads to the basement now."

"But why would someone make the stairs smaller, especially when all they did with the empty space was wall it over?"

"I don't know," Gideon admitted, heading back through the house to the basement stairs. "But I'm hoping we can find out."

He set down his mug of coffee and took the tools they'd bought as he headed down the stairs. Maggie had her flashlight back on, its bright beam leading the way for his feet to follow.

A couple of quick measurements confirmed his suspicions. "There's a lot more space behind this wall than what's taken up by the stairwell, you just don't notice it from the other side because the stairs themselves disguise the space."

"That's exactly the kind of thing my dad would have noticed." Maggie's fingers touched the cement wall. "How are we going to get inside? This thing looks solid."

"Let's try the other side in the back room. The walls in there have that old wallpaper on them. I never paid much attention to what the material was underneath."

They hurried through the dark hallway to the large back storage room. Gideon pressed his hands against the back wall, then rapped against it a few times with his knuckles.

"Hollow?" Maggie asked.

"Not only that, I think this wall is made of some old sort of paneling. Anyway, it feels like lightweight wood composite. Who knows how old it is?" As he spoke, he felt along the wall for a seam, finally encountering one in the very corner of the room. He pried his fingers into the joint, but the old paneling wouldn't budge.

"Crowbar?" Maggie pulled the tool from the bag they'd brought down with them.

"Thanks." Inserting the end into the crack, Gideon eased the old wood back, surprised that it seemed to be securely attached. That didn't mesh with his theory of an accessible space behind the wall. He grumbled impatiently as he tried the crowbar at several angles, to no avail.

"Maybe it has a latch or something," Maggie suggested, slipping past him when he stepped back to survey the wall.

With her smaller, more nimble fingers, Maggie felt along the seam starting at the floor. Two-thirds of the way up she stopped. "Found it." She squeezed her fingers into the small space.

Gideon reached forward and stopped her hand. "Careful. Slowly—there could be bats." He didn't want to have to repeat what had happened the last time they'd opened up a wall.

But as they held on to the panel and swung it cautiously outward, nothing flew out to meet them. Maggie pointed the beam of her flashlight into the musty hole, revealing a slimy space with a layer of bat guano and thick, moldering dust. Her light reflected off something shiny, and she aimed the beam at the spot.

It took Gideon a moment to realize what she'd found. In the midst of the moldering old guano sat a large box, apparently made of wood, probably a good six feet long, which more or less filled the floor of the hidden room. Maggie's light had flashed across a brass latch that had been wiped clean at some point in the not-so-distant past.

"Oh, that's creepy," Maggie confessed, taking a step back.

Still eager to assess their find, Gideon let his arm fall around Maggie's shoulders, and he pulled her against him as he leaned forward to look past her. "Is it a coffin?"

Maggie's body trembled under his hand as a shudder rippled through her. "It looks like it. It looks like it's been here a long time." She sounded dismayed. "Oh, and it smells so terrible."

For the first time, Gideon realized she was right. More than the musty scent of decay, more than the earthy smell of the rotting bat guano, he smelled something acrid, the stench strong and offensive. It brought tears to his eyes.

"Smoke!" Maggie said in a sharp whisper just as Gideon recognized the smell.

"Lots of smoke," he agreed. "It's coming in through the door." He rushed back to the dark hallway, but there the smoke was so thick he couldn't see anything. They didn't dare try to make it out that way—not with the armoire still blocking the cellar door. Gideon pulled the hallway door shut, effectively limiting the amount of smoke that made it into the room. The move bought them some time, but they still needed out.

"The window." Maggie crossed the room to the narrow basement window that looked out onto the underside of some bushes that ran along the house outside. She was too short to reach the sill. "Help me, quick!"

Gideon rushed over and pulled the aging window from its frame, then punched out the screen onto the snow outside. "Out you go," he said, not waiting for Maggie to give her permission before he bent down and wrapped his arms around her knees, hoisting her toward the window.

She squealed but didn't fight him. Instead she grabbed the window frame and wriggled her way through.

"Come on, Gideon, get out of there," she called down the instant she was free of the window.

"Call the fire department," he shouted back up as he pulled a dresser toward the window to step up on. "And stand clear!"

Using the dresser like a step stool, he hefted himself up and pulled his body through the window onto the cold snow outside. To his relief, he saw Maggie standing on the other side of the bushes, her cell phone already at her ear as she quickly relayed their situation. She had her arms wrapped around her shoulders as she shivered in the frigid air.

Gideon was at her side in a moment. He pulled her farther away from the house and draped his arms around her shivering shoulders. While she finished the phone call, Gideon tried to assess the scope of the fire.

Thick smoke poured from the back of the house. If

he hadn't already turned off the outdoor spigots for the winter, Gideon might have tried to turn a hose on the fire himself. Instead, all he could do was stand back and watch the bright orange flames lick up the side of the building.

Maggie closed her phone and looked up at him. "I don't know if you can still smell it," she began in a wavering voice.

"Gasoline?" Gideon asked, and saw confirmation in her eyes.

"Somebody lit our house on fire." Maggie's voice sounded strained, but not so strained that Gideon could possibly miss the pronoun she'd used.

Our house.

She was under stress. He shouldn't read too much into it. And yet, he felt that way about the house—as if it was theirs, together, not just their project to work on together, but their house.

And somebody had lit it on fire.

"Do you think—" Maggie's voice continued to shake, and Gideon tightened his arms around her "—do you think they were watching us?"

"Like they watched your father?"

"If they knew when he found the casket…" Her voice trailed away as the first fire truck pulled into the yard, its sirens blazing, men leaping out and starting to work before the vehicle even came to a complete stop.

"Is anyone still inside?" A fireman shouted.

"Not that I know of." Maggie looked to Gideon for confirmation. "Kayla left for work earlier. No one should be around."

"Not unless the person who set the fire stuck around."

* * *

Maggie felt a clenching in her stomach that was more than the combination of hunger and pain from the smoke in her lungs.

This was bigger than stolen keys and footprints in the snow. Bigger even than the possibility that her father's death might not have been an accident. Someone had tried to burn down her house. Someone had tried to kill them.

She watched as the firemen hurried to put out the blaze, until the charred backside of the house stood stark and black against the snow-covered land all around it. Gideon kept his arms around her, and Maggie laced her fingers through his. She told herself it was just because of the cold, but the blankets the firemen had tossed them were more than enough to keep them warm.

But she wasn't about to push Gideon away. She needed the strength and security he offered. She needed to feel his strong arms enfolding her, shielding her from whatever else was out there. While the fire investigator quizzed them on what had happened, Maggie stayed close to Gideon. She needed the reassurance his presence gave her.

As they spoke, she felt his shoulders stiffen and his breath catch. She looked up and followed the direction of his eyes to where a sheriff's cruiser pulled in behind the fire truck.

Deputy Bernie Gills stepped out. Maggie understood why Gideon had tensed. Bernie was the deputy who'd accused Gideon of stealing his Taser. Bernie was the guy who'd openly told Gideon he hoped he went to prison.

"Have a little fire here, did we?" the deputy asked. "This place fully insured?"

"Yes," Maggie answered hesitantly, unsure why the deputy had asked.

"Hard to collect if it doesn't burn all the way down, isn't it?" Bernie laughed, and Maggie realized what the man was openly hinting at. Did he think they'd tried to burn the house down to collect the insurance money?

Gideon let go of Maggie and stepped toward the deputy. "For your information," he began, but the uniformed officer spun back around to face him.

"If I want any information from you, I'll ask for it," he snapped, then looked pleased when Gideon fell silent. The deputy turned to the fire investigator. "Let me guess. Arson?"

"Looks like it."

Bernie rubbed his hands together. "Ooh, this just gets better and better."

Maggie watched the uniformed man walk toward the house. She felt cold now that Gideon had stepped away from her, though she still held the blanket tight around her shoulders and its insulating thickness kept her body warm. The cold she felt originated in the pit of her stomach and worked its way up with every frightened beat of her heart. Bernie already thought Gideon was a guilty man. Between the possible motive and the dozens of Gideon's fingerprints the officer would no doubt find all over the crime scene, he'd probably be able to concoct a tight enough case against him.

Which meant even if Gideon was cleared of the drug charges his brother had framed him with, he might still end up going to prison.

THIRTEEN

Gideon couldn't stand it. Too much had gone wrong too quickly. The situation was spiraling out of his control. What had the Bible said? *He who trusts in Me will never be condemned.*

He didn't want to put God to the test, but it would take a miracle for him to emerge from this a free man. "Can I borrow your phone?" he asked Maggie. He'd left his inside the house, and the fire crew still hadn't cleared them to go back inside.

"Sure." Maggie handed it over with questions in her eyes.

"I'm going to call Sheriff Walker," he explained. "I want somebody to take a look at what we found in the basement. I have a feeling everything hinges on that."

"Good idea," Maggie encouraged him.

To his relief, instead of telling him to share their find with Bernie, Kim Walker agreed to come by and take a look herself. Gideon didn't know much about the young woman, but he knew Bernie already had it in for him. He could only pray Sheriff Walker would be open to the possibility that he might actually be innocent.

By the time Kim arrived, Gideon had received permission to reenter the house.

"Structurally she looks sound," the fire chief had explained. "The siding on the back of the house is a total loss, but the studs themselves are fine. Gasoline vapors burn outward," he offered, meeting Gideon's eyes with a meaningful look.

Gideon had worked with the man on several cases over the years, but he couldn't read what this look meant. Did the fire chief think he was guilty of setting the house on fire? His words seemed to carry more meaning than a simple relaying of facts. Gideon didn't have time to sort it out. They had a coffin to open.

He attempted to update the new sheriff on his suspicions as they headed to the basement. He didn't get very far.

"Glen Arnold's death was ruled accidental," Kim corrected him with a glance to Maggie, who'd followed them down the stairs.

"I know," Gideon acknowledged patiently. He needed this woman on his side. He just wasn't sure how to get her there. "Have you had a chance to review the report?"

"The case was closed by the time I started."

"I understand." Gideon focused on keeping his tone light. It wasn't easy. "If you get a chance to look at the file, you'll see there were several suspicious elements to the case. I received a phone call from Glen twenty minutes prior to finding his body. He told me he'd discovered something suspicious inside the house. He asked me to come take a look, but he wouldn't tell me what he'd found—it was something I wouldn't believe until I saw it, according to Glen."

Kim scowled. "I was unaware of that."

"In addition to the phone call, Glen's pockets were turned out when I discovered him."

"As though they'd been searched?" Kim clarified.

"That's what it looked like to me."

"But all of this happened months ago," the interim sheriff clarified. "So why bring me down here today?"

Gideon swallowed back the lump that had inexplicably risen in his throat. He glanced at Maggie, who gave him a small, encouraging smile. "Maggie and I found something in this back room today which we think may have been the item Glen Arnold spoke of in his final phone call to me. Before we were able to look any closer, we discovered the house was on fire and we escaped through the window."

Kim's eyes widened. "What did you find?" she asked.

"A casket."

Maggie hovered nearby as Gideon pulled the heavy-looking box from the space and set it in the middle of the room. He scowled as he looked down at the lock. "I wish we had the key to this thing."

"Someone did," Kim observed, pointing with her pen at the back of the casket where the hinged lid was joined to the body. "The encrusted materials were disturbed at some point, indicating that the lid was opened."

Intrigued, Maggie asked, "Can you tell how long ago that was?"

"Hard to say. If the casket was sitting undisturbed in the wall, it may have been weeks or even months ago."

Maggie's heart thumped hard inside her. "Do you think my dad may have opened it?" She peered in a little closer at the brass lock plate and gave a gasp.

Gideon met her eyes.

"It's the same scrolling design that was on the brass key."

Sheriff Walker looked back and forth between the two of them. "What key?"

"Glen left a key in the glove compartment of his truck.

Maggie found it and placed it on her key ring, but it was stolen Saturday."

"Did you report the theft?" the sheriff asked.

"No," Gideon admitted.

Maggie didn't see what that had to do with anything. "My father's pockets were turned out as though they were searched. His killer obviously thought he had something on him. Something that they wanted. They wrote 'GIVE IT BACK' on the Dumpster."

"Possibly indicating the key," Gideon continued.

"If it hadn't been stolen we could have opened the coffin." Maggie heard the regret she felt echoing in her words.

Both former and current sheriffs looked at her with sympathy.

"It's certainly a possibility," Kim agreed. "But for now, I still think we can get this thing opened up."

"How?" Maggie asked.

"I don't want to damage the evidence any more than necessary," Kim noted. "We need a locksmith."

"Bernie can probably handle it," Gideon offered.

Both women looked at him.

"Do you realize Bernie thinks you're guilty?" Kim asked.

Gideon nodded. "I'm not guilty. I don't have anything to hide from Bernie or anyone else. We need this casket opened and Bernie has the skills to do it. Even better, he should still be outside."

Kim nodded solemnly. "I'll call him in."

"Thank you." Gideon nodded. "With your permission, I'll bring this upstairs where we should have more light."

Maggie insisted Gideon not try to lift the casket himself.

"It's not that heavy," he protested.

"But it *is* cumbersome, and we don't want to disturb the contents," she pointed out, relieved when he relented to letting her ask some of the firefighters to help them carry the box outside. They set it down on the patio in the snow and Bernie got right to work.

"Not a hard one," Bernie announced when he popped the lock open a few moments later, lifting the upper-body portion of the hinged lid.

As Maggie had assumed, the inside was lined with satiny fabric much like any other casket. There was indeed a body inside, presumably female from the clothing, though with all the curious firemen gathered around, it took a moment before Maggie caught sight of the woman's embalmed face.

"Lorna Creel!" she gasped. She hadn't seen the woman in years, not since she'd moved away from Holyoake after high school, but she'd recognize that hawkish nose any-where, even in death.

"Yeah, looks like her," another fireman, a lifetime local if Maggie recalled correctly, concurred with Maggie's assessment. "I didn't know she was dead."

"Well, she's certainly not alive," Bernie remarked gruffly, setting the lid shut again.

Maggie was glad she didn't have to look at the embalmed body any longer. She tried not to shudder, but the implications of their find hit her with sudden force. She staggered backward a few steps. "Oh, no," she said softly.

Kim gave her a concerned look. "What is it?"

Still mostly stunned by what she'd realized, it took Maggie a moment to speak. "The bank foreclosed on Lorna because she wasn't making her house payments. That's how my father bought this house—out of foreclosure from the bank. But they shouldn't have foreclosed on her if she was dead." The words came rambling from her lips as quickly as she thought them.

"That's right," another fireman agreed. "Her kids should have inherited it. She had, what, a daughter and a son?"

"Linda was the girl's name," another fireman added.

"And Dan was her son. I went to school with him," the first fireman finished.

"You'd think the bank would have done a more thorough investigation before they foreclosed," Kim said as she stepped away from the casket.

"I heard they sent letters that went unanswered," Maggie recalled from what her Realtor had told her.

"Dead people don't answer their mail," another fireman observed.

"Yeah, and they don't make their mortgage payments, either," Bernie straightened and wiped his hands off on his slacks. "This case just keeps getting weirder."

Maggie wondered if perhaps Bernie's comment indicated he'd begun to doubt his earlier theory that Gideon was behind everything. Gideon hadn't had any connection to the house until he'd started working on it with her. And the body had clearly been there much longer than that.

"How long do you think she's been dead?" Maggie asked.

No one spoke, though a couple of the firemen shrugged.

"Hard to tell without an autopsy," Gideon answered after some silence. "Embalmed bodies continue to look much the same for decades—the embalming process takes care of that. I've witnessed exhumations of bodies that had been in the grave for years. If it weren't for their old-fashioned clothing, you'd have guessed they died the day before."

Maggie swallowed and looked back at the closed casket. The woman inside had been wearing an upscale mauve suit—the kind that had been popular among older ladies for decades. The suit itself wouldn't help them date the body. "So are we going to have an autopsy?" Maggie wasn't sure how that process worked.

"I'm sure we'll need to, especially if there's no record of her death," Kim agreed. "We'll try to track down Lorna Creel's next of kin to find out if they know anything about her death or how she ended up in the basement of this house."

"I have her son's contact information inside the house," Gideon volunteered.

"Perfect." Kim smiled. "And doesn't her daughter live around here, too?"

"Yeah." Bernie made a musing face. "Seems to me Lorna had Linda when she was a lot younger, before her husband died. Then Dan came along, oh, after the older girl had graduated from high school, I think."

"Were they really that far apart in age?" a fireman asked.

"That sounds right to me," Maggie agreed. "I used to babysit Dan Creel after his sister was married. And I always thought Lorna was awfully old to have a son so young." She remembered how crotchety the woman had been back then, and shuddered to think the bitter woman's embalmed body had been hidden inside her house all this time.

Kim nodded and jotted some notes on a pad. "We'll get in touch with Dan and Linda to sort this out. They should be able to tell us when their mother died. Hopefully they know what her body was doing in this basement, too."

* * *

Maggie was relieved once everyone had finally left and the body was en route to an autopsy. The only good news that had come out of the afternoon was that the fire investigator found an empty gasoline can near the edge of the woods. Though the backyard of the house on Shady Oak Lane had been thoroughly trampled by the time the firefighters put out the blaze, they discovered several footprints near where the empty container was found. The footprints were similar in size to the ones Maggie and Gideon had followed through the woods before, and were much too small to belong to Dan Creel.

Though Maggie thought she recognized the gas can from one she'd seen previously in the shed, neither she nor Gideon had ever touched it, so Maggie was optimistic any fingerprints found would divert suspicion away from either of them. A quick check of the shed revealed more footprints on the dusty floor and no sign of a gas can where Maggie thought she'd spotted one weeks before, leading her to believe the arsonist had grabbed the gas from the shed to dump on the fire.

"It makes me think it was an impromptu fire," Maggie mused aloud as she and Gideon returned to the kitchen after the investigators had wrapped up their search.

Gideon's eyes narrowed. "My guess is the arsonist knew the gas can was there ahead of time. He may have been thinking about lighting a fire for some time, but didn't resort to starting the blaze until we found the casket."

As the meaning of Gideon's words sank in, Maggie hugged herself tightly against the cold she felt both inside and out. Had her father's killer been watching them that closely? And if Gideon was right about criminal behavior escalating, what might the killer resort to next?

* * *

After the long day they'd had dealing with the fire and the casket, Gideon offered to take Maggie and Kayla out for pizza that evening. Though Gideon knew Maggie usually preferred to eat at home, she accepted his invitation with a happy smile. It seemed he wasn't the only one who was eager to get away from the house on Shady Oak Lane.

Kayla gave them a hard time about trying to burn the house down while she was at work, but even though Maggie chuckled at her accusations, the worry shined through on her face and in her voice. Fortunately Kayla spotted some friends at the pizza place and joined them at their table to chat. Her carefree laughter echoed through the restaurant.

A shadowed smile fleeted across Maggie's face at the sound of Kayla's laughter, but concern quickly replaced it.

"Worried you might lose the house?" Gideon asked gently while they waited for their pizza.

Maggie fiddled with her straw wrapper, tying it in knots until it crumbled away in bits. "I suppose I shouldn't be. I didn't ask for that house. I didn't want to deal with it. And yet..." Her eyes met his, and her voice dropped away.

Gideon let a gentle smile rise to his eyes. Maggie was so pretty, even worried like she was. She'd taken some of Kayla's makeup tips and toned them down somehow. He wasn't sure what she'd done but she looked good, in spite of the concern that etched her expression. "The place kind of grows on you, doesn't it?"

She shrugged. "I was starting to look forward to seeing it all fixed up. Those books you bought had some great ideas in them. With time and a little investment it could look amazing." She shook her head. "Not that I have time to spend on the project. I should be relieved that it won't be my concern anymore."

A thought kept flitting through Gideon's mind. He told himself it was a stupid idea, but it wouldn't go away. "Maybe you could offer to buy it from them," he said, and immediately wished he hadn't. Why would Maggie want to spend money on a house she'd never wanted in the first place? He knew she'd been hoping to make enough profit to make a large donation to the hospital where she worked in Kansas City in order to have a room named after her father. If she spent all her money on the house that would never happen.

At least she was polite enough not to chide him for his foolish idea. Instead she laughed it off. "That wouldn't make much sense, would it?" she asked as she chuckled.

Gideon laughed along with her, pleased that he'd at least brought a smile to her face after all the difficulties she'd been through that day.

His phone rang a moment later, and he answered, relieved to hear Kim Walker's voice on the other end. "Yes, Sheriff Walker. Thanks for getting back to me. Do you have some answers for us?"

"Only more questions," she apologized. "We weren't able to reach Linda, but we got in touch with Dan. His plane just touched down in Seattle. He won't be able to make it back to ID the body for at least another sixteen hours."

Gideon let a groan escape his lips. Maggie reached for his hand, and he held the phone out from his ear, notching up the volume so Maggie could listen in. They leaned their heads together across the small table as the interim sheriff's voice carried through clear and strong.

"We explained the situation to Dan and he seemed

bewildered. He claims he spoke to his mother on the phone as recently as August."

"Just this past August?" Gideon clarified. "As in three months ago, or so?"

"That's what he claimed. He said he couldn't recall the exact date, but he'd try to remember and get back to us."

"Is he absolutely certain the person he spoke to on the phone was his mother?"

Kim was silent for a moment. "I didn't think to ask him that. I'm sorry, his answer took me by surprise, and our phone connection wasn't the best."

"That's okay," Gideon was quick to assure her. "I'm glad you were able to learn what you did. But it would be helpful to know."

"I'm sure it would." Her tone said she was ready to end the call. "That's all I have right now."

"I appreciate what you've done. Call me if you learn anything else. I'll do the same." With another word of thanks, Gideon snapped the phone shut and looked into Maggie's frightened eyes.

"August?" she repeated. "That doesn't make any sense. My father bought the house in June. How could her body possibly get into a casket in the basement—"

Before she had a chance to get too worked up, Gideon squeezed her hand. "It can't be right. It just can't. That casket had to have been down there for longer than that. I'd say a lot longer just based on the way it looked."

His words calmed the fear-filled look in her eyes. "Then who did Dan talk to on the phone?"

"I don't know. Do you think he was lying?"

"Little Danny Creel?" Maggie's expression softened. "He was always such a good kid, with such a gentle heart. I'd hate to think he's the one behind all this."

"I know." Gideon understood her reluctance to pin

everything on Dan. The man certainly hadn't acted like a criminal that morning. "Maybe he got his facts mixed up. Maybe he only thinks the woman he spoke to was his mother. Whoever put that casket behind the wall was obviously trying to hide something."

"We've got to find out who it was," Maggie said with determination in her eyes. "I can't help but believe that whoever put the casket behind the wall was the same person who killed my father." She shook her head remorsefully. "I just wish I knew who. And why?"

FOURTEEN

In spite of the long day they'd been through, Maggie didn't want to go to bed that evening. "Want to take another look in the basement with me?" she offered Gideon.

"Let me grab my flashlight."

Kayla clucked her tongue at them. "You two can look for more hidden rooms if you want," she said, stretching, "but I've got to work another early shift tomorrow, and I need my beauty sleep. Good night."

As Kayla shuffled off to the bedroom, Gideon returned with a high-powered flashlight and accompanied Maggie down the stairs. The sheriff's team had taken the casket and its contents but had barely looked into the hidden room at all. Maggie got the sense Gideon was determined to do a thorough search. They might yet find a clue that could lead them to her father's killer, or at least to the person who'd left poor Lorna behind the wall.

They worked in silence, scraping out the bat guano and methodically sifting through it. As always when she worked closely with Gideon Bromley, Maggie felt secure in their silent camaraderie. They worked well as a team. It was something she'd always appreciate about him, even after she left Holyoake.

She sniffled back a tear before she realized how

emotional she'd become at the thought of moving away from Gideon. She hoped the usually silent man would stay quiet about it, but he settled back on his haunches with his wrists resting on his knees and his gloved hands held out away from his jeans.

"Is this bothering you?" he asked.

Unable to admit why she'd sniffled, Maggie confessed to the other emotional thought that had been running through her head while they worked. "Do you think this little room was one of the last things my father saw before he died?"

Rather than deny it, Gideon surprised her by noting, "It was almost the last thing we saw." He cleared his throat and relaxed into a cross-legged sitting position on the floor, their work cleaning out the little room all but completed. "Kind of makes you think about how short life is, about how quickly everything can change."

Maggie felt the weight of her impending move crushing against her heart, and settled back onto the floor with her knee near his. "It makes me think about what's real and what's not, about what really matters and what doesn't."

They stared into the tiny room for a while longer before Maggie explained, "For nearly twenty years I didn't think I could show my face in Holyoake because everybody here blamed my father for making Kayla sick. But it was her own father's fault she got sick. It was *his* lies that led people to think me and my dad were bad people. It wasn't real, but it made my high-school years torture, and then I left and never came back."

"You felt condemned," Gideon concluded softly.

"Yes." She let out the word with a heart-heavy sigh.

"'But now there is no condemnation for those of us who are in Christ Jesus,'" Gideon quoted, "'because through

Christ Jesus the law of the Spirit of life sets us free from the law of sin and death.'"

Maggie looked at him with wide eyes. "Where—?" she started to ask.

But Gideon quickly offered, "Romans. Didn't realize I'd memorized it all the way. I just had to read it so many times before I could really accept it was true."

"'There is no condemnation for those of us who are in Christ Jesus,'" Maggie murmured, in awe of how precisely the scripture spoke to her hurt. She gulped back a cry of pain as her wounded heart tore. "I felt condemned for so long. And it was a *lie*."

Gideon snapped off his dirty gloves. When Maggie did the same, he took her hand in his. "I know how you feel."

Maggie squeezed his hand, realizing he knew exactly how she felt and more. Though she'd lived in self-imposed exile for years, Gideon faced the very real possibility of a long prison sentence for his brother's lies. Bruce Bromley had made both of them feel condemned.

Another sob tore at her, and she bit it back, letting the tears run silently down her cheeks. Though she wished she could stay there holding Gideon's hand forever, she knew she needed to wipe away her tears, so she dropped his hand and stood, looking around for something to swab at her cheeks with.

Just as he had so often before, Gideon seemed to instinctively know what Maggie needed. He rose and reached toward her with his hand extended as though to wipe away her tears. At the last second he caught himself and looked at his hand, as though suspicious that it may have become contaminated in spite of the gloves he'd worn.

Then, to Maggie's surprise, Gideon leaned toward her

and softly brushed her left cheek with his lips. She closed her eyes and relished his touch, leaning into him as he buried his forehead against her moist cheek and kissed the tears along her lower jawline.

"Gideon?" she whispered, unsure what his gesture meant.

He didn't respond with words, but pulled her tight against his chest, where the last of her tears soaked into the softness of his shirt. Maggie buried her face in his shoulder and sniffled away the last of her tears. How could she cry when Gideon was holding her so tenderly? She stood there, leaning against him while he held her tight, for several long minutes until his arms relaxed and he began to step away.

"It's late," he said simply.

Maggie nodded and found her voice. "We should probably call it a night."

He led the way back up the stairs and they parted ways.

Maggie headed for bed without seeing Gideon again, but her mind was filled with thoughts of him, especially the embrace they'd shared. What did it mean? Too exhausted by all the events of the day to sort it out, she fell asleep warmed by the memory of what it felt like to be in Gideon's arms.

Gideon couldn't fall asleep. His body was tired, but the agitation he felt wouldn't let him relax. First there was the mystery surrounding everything that had taken place at the house on Shady Oak Lane. Like a riddle, all the pieces seemed to hint at some hidden answer that felt as if it was just beyond him. Though he had no idea how Lorna Creel's embalmed body had come to rest in the hidden room in the basement, or why anyone would steal random objects from the Dumpster just to hide them in the woods, Gideon was certain of one thing: Glen Arnold had been murdered. And it only seemed fair to assume that whoever had killed Maggie's father was behind the fire, as well.

While the enigma taunted him with its mystifying clues, Gideon wrestled with an issue that, if possible, hit even closer to his heart. Everything he'd said to Maggie while they'd shared that unforgettable time in the basement only made him realize even more how much both of them had been injured by his brother's drug crimes. Not only had his brother framed him for the crime, but he'd framed Glen and Maggie, forcing them to bear the stigma of Kayla's illness all those years.

It wasn't fair that his brother should get away with his crimes. As long as Bruce Bromley insisted on his own innocence, both Gideon and Maggie would continue to pay for his illegal actions. Gideon could yet end up in prison. Worse yet, Gideon now realized, Bruce had been behind Maggie's leaving town all those years before. As long as people continued to believe the lies Bruce had told them, Maggie would never want to live in Holyoake. And Gideon realized he wanted Maggie to be able to stay. He cared about her.

Which left Gideon with only one option. He *had* to convince his brother to confess—if not for all of his crimes, then at least for producing the fumes that had made Kayla ill all those years ago. It wasn't fair the guilt that Maggie had been saddled with. And Gideon loved her too much to stand by and watch as she continued to pay the price for what his brother had done.

Maggie was awakened by a creaking sound. She lay still a moment, waiting for the sound to come again, then heard the unmistakable sound of the floorboards creaking in the hallway upstairs. Squinting over at Kayla's bed, she saw that the young woman was gone, her coverlet tucked neatly around her pillow the way she always left it made. Shoving on her glasses so she could see the clock, Maggie realized it was after six in the morning. Kayla's shift at the hospital had already started. She wouldn't even be home, let alone walking around upstairs.

Which left Gideon, and Maggie wasn't sure she was ready to face him after what they'd shared the evening before. What if he was embarrassed by it, or worse yet, what if he regretted what he'd done?

"Maggie?" Gideon whispered from the other side of her door.

"Yes?" Whether she was ready to face him or not, she couldn't really hide from him. But he'd never disturbed her at such an early hour before. What was going on?

"Did you leave the attic light on?"

"Attic light?" she repeated, uncertain she'd heard him correctly. She never went in the attic, so how could she have left the light on? With her curiosity prodding her, she hopped out of bed and quickly pulled on some clothes while Gideon explained his inquiry from the other side of the door.

"I woke up when I heard Kayla starting her car to go to work. I couldn't get back to sleep, so I decided to just get up. When I stepped into the hallway, I noticed a ring of light around the attic door like someone had left the light on up there. But I haven't been in the attic in weeks, and I don't think Kayla has gone anywhere near it, either."

By the time Gideon finished his story, Maggie was mostly dressed, and she simultaneously pulled the door open while trying to put her last shoe on. She hopped on one foot while wrestling with the sneaker. "I haven't gone up there in weeks, either. Even if we had left the light on weeks ago, surely we'd have noticed it before now, or the bulb would have burned out. Did any of the fire investigators go up there yesterday?"

Gideon placed his hands on her shoulders and stilled her hopping while she settled her sneaker onto her foot. A warm reminder of their embrace the evening before flooded her at his touch. But the chill behind his next words chased away the warmth she felt.

"We don't know where the arsonist went after he set the fire, or even if he was working alone. And we still haven't changed the locks since your keys were stolen."

"Do you think the arsonist might have gone into the attic?" Maggie asked, lowering her voice instinctively.

"It's possible," Gideon nodded solemnly.

Maggie swallowed. "Do you think they might even still be up there?"

Gideon nodded again.

"Do you think we should call the sheriff?"

Hesitation flashed across Gideon's face. "If we're wrong, we'll look foolish."

"But Sheriff Walker knows something happened here. I think she believes everything we've told her so far, no matter what Bernie Gills might think."

"I'd like her to continue to believe us, too," Gideon answered. "If we cry wolf she'll begin to doubt the trust she's placed in us. I don't think we can afford to do anything that might instill any further doubt in her mind. It's just a light. It could be a wiring problem for all we know."

Maggie glanced toward the stairs that led to the second floor. The pull-down hatch that held the attic stairs was located on the ceiling in the second-floor hallway, well beyond her line of sight. But she could picture it clearly and could imagine what the rim of light would look like cutting through the predawn darkness.

"So you think we should check it out ourselves?" She looked into his eyes, more aware than ever of how close he stood to her, and how steady his hands felt on her shoulders.

"I don't think we have any choice," he said finally. "I'll go first. I want you to stay on the second floor, out of sight but where you can still hear me, with your hand on the phone. If I don't give you an all clear within thirty seconds, call for help. Don't come looking for me."

Maggie gulped. "Do you think someone may be lying in wait for us?"

"It's possible." His eyes softened and he slid his hands down her arms until he held her hands in his secure grasp. "Do you want to pray before we go up there?"

Whatever lingering doubts Maggie might have had about Gideon's faith disappeared as she folded her hands in his and he started a prayer, not just for their safety, but that God's justice would prevail and her father's killer would finally be caught. It wasn't a fancy prayer, but she knew his words came straight from his heart, and they spoke to every fear that haunted her. "We know You don't condemn us, Lord," Gideon prayed. "We pray that everything would be resolved."

"And keep Gideon safe, Lord," Maggie cut in when she felt as though Gideon was about to end the prayer. "Keep him perfectly safe in Your hands."

"Amen."

They ended the prayer together, and Gideon quickly dropped her hands. "Let me grab a flashlight," he said, disappearing up the stairs. By the time Maggie joined him on the second floor, Gideon stood, flashlight in hand, below the hatch in the ceiling that led to the attic. A golden rim of artificial light edged the opening.

Maggie thought of something. "Wasn't it dark in the hallway when you went to bed last night?"

Gideon spun to face her and narrowed his eyes. "If a light was on in the attic then, I should have seen it. I could hardly have missed it."

Fear swirled in Maggie's stomach. She thought about asking Gideon not to try the door after all, but he guided her toward the open doorway of the almost finished bedroom next to his. "Stay in here out of sight behind the door. You have your phone ready?"

She held it up for him to see.

"Good. Give me thirty seconds. If I don't give you an all clear, then call 911."

Maggie gripped the phone and nodded. She felt a part of her heart go with him as Gideon crept back into the hallway and slowly lowered the pull-down hatch that housed the collapsible stairs to the attic. The lightweight wooden frame creaked slightly under his weight as he cautiously climbed upward.

Though she knew she was supposed to stay out of sight, Maggie couldn't help but peek just around the rim of the doorway as she waited to see what would befall the former sheriff. He made it safely up the stairs and his feet disappeared from her view.

Forcing herself to count slowly on her way up to thirty, Maggie nearly jumped when Gideon called down, "All clear!"

"You're sure?" Maggie questioned him, still tightly gripping her phone.

"Unless someone is hiding in a dresser drawer."

"Or in another secret room," Maggie offered with as

much of a joking tone as she could muster as she climbed the steps to join him.

Their eyes met as she finished her sentence, and she saw a spark of realization alight on Gideon's face at her words. He gave her a meaningful look.

She raised her eyebrows. "Is it possible?" she began.

Gideon spun around, scowling at the walls.

With her heart thumping madly inside her, Maggie reviewed what they'd learned about the hidden spaces they'd discovered so far. "The back stairs to the basement may have been a larger stairway once."

Gideon picked up where Maggie left off. "We don't know why they were rebuilt to take up less space. It doesn't seem to make any sense if the space gained was just walled off."

"But what if the stairs didn't just go to the basement? What if my father discovered remnants of a back stairway while he was gutting the second floor? What if the back stairs originally went all the way from the attic to the cellar?"

Gideon snapped his fingers. "That may have been what led him to suspect a hidden room in the basement in the first place." He crossed the room and placed his hands on a vertical portion of the wall. While most of the attic space was covered with old wallpaper that swept down at an angle that followed the contour of the roof, that section of wall went from a higher part of the ceiling in a straight drop to the floor.

Placing his ear against the crumbling brown wallpaper, Gideon rapped the wall with his knuckles. "Hollow," he said, shaking his head.

"Do you want your sledgehammer?" Maggie asked, eager to learn what was on the other side of the wall.

But Gideon was already sweeping his hands over the

space, clearly looking for a seam. "There was a latch on the basement wall," he muttered.

Maggie joined him, prodding the soft wallboard, her fingers instinctively flying to the corresponding point where she'd found the latch on the basement wall. "Got it," she said, flicking the latch open with a practiced motion.

Gideon's hands immediately covered hers. "Careful," he said, holding her hands still. "There could be bats."

"Want me to open a window so they can escape?" Maggie asked, recalling how the open door of the kitchen had allowed the flying creatures a means of escaping the last time they'd inadvertently disturbed their lair.

"Good idea."

Crossing the room to the nearest window, which stretched from just above the floor to the maximum height allowed by the rear gable, Maggie unlatched the old clasps that held the glass frame in place. "This old thing doesn't even have a screen," Maggie noted as she set the freed pane to the side, leaving a gaping hole for the winter air to rush in.

"That will give any bats plenty of room to escape." Gideon sounded pleased. "We can close it again in a minute." His arm muscles rippled under the snug T-shirt he wore as he held onto the wall. "Ready?"

Maggie crouched behind him, ready to duck if any bats flew out. "Ready." She tensed as Gideon moved beside her, opening the wall like a door. Nothing flew out.

"No bats?" she cautiously peeked around him.

"I think they're hibernating," Gideon said, pointing to clusters of the cozy-looking creatures that nestled upside down along the ceiling of the small space.

With an involuntary shudder, Maggie looked away from the unruffled creatures to the rest of the space they'd uncovered. At the same time, Gideon flashed the beam of his light downward across a wooden box. Much like the one they'd found in the basement, this box too was also covered with a thick layer of bat guano. But in spite of the hundreds of bats that hibernated above it, the brass keyhole plate was wiped clean. It bore the same scrolling design that had adorned the lock plate on the coffin.

"It's too small to be a casket," Maggie observed, trying to reassure herself that no other embalmed bodies lay inside.

"Far too small," Gideon agreed.

"I'm going to call the sheriff's office." Maggie opened her phone again. "Maybe Bernie Gills can—"

A bright flash of white shot across Maggie's field of vision, and the next thing she knew she was lying on her back, looking up into the leering face of Lorna Creel, who Maggie realized was actually bigger than the woman they'd found in the casket.

And unlike the body they'd discovered, Lorna Creel was definitely not dead.

FIFTEEN

Gideon spun around just in time to see the flash of the weapon that had taken Maggie down. It was Bernie's Taser, no doubt about it. He recognized Lorna immediately, and realized the woman in the casket, though very much like Lorna in appearance, had probably been older and smaller than the looming figure who stood over them both, loading an air cartridge into the Taser. She must have used the Taser on Maggie in drive stun mode, which was slightly less painful, but still unconscionable in Gideon's mind.

"You're not calling anyone!" Lorna shouted, kicking Maggie's phone away.

Furious that the woman had hurt Maggie, Gideon rushed at Lorna, his only thought to keep her away from Maggie.

He remembered the air cartridge she'd loaded into the Taser a split second before the barbs struck his shoulder. Pain speared through his body and his muscles clenched. Time seemed to slow down as he fought to move in spite of his tight, unresponsive muscles.

"Stop! You're hurting him!" Maggie's voice penetrated the stupor, and a moment later, like coming up for air after far too long underwater, he felt the hold on his body release as suddenly as it had begun, and he realized Maggie had rushed the woman.

"Maggie, no," Gideon gasped, hardly able to make his voice respond. He rolled onto his side and attempted to stand, but his muscles continued to throb from the prolonged shock they'd received. He knew Maggie was in danger. Though Lorna had discharged the air cartridge on him, she could still use the Taser on Maggie in drive stun mode.

Recalling the barbs in his chest, Gideon swiped at them, pulling them loose, and finally managed to gain his feet in time to see Maggie struggling with Lorna several feet away, attempting to wrestle the Taser from her hands. Maggie was no match for the larger woman.

Gideon forced his feet to obey and bit back a scream as a pins-and-needles sensation speared up from his feet through his traumatized leg muscles. He had to get Lorna away from Maggie. He couldn't let her be hurt again.

He was less than a foot away when the crazed woman spun around, her expression a hideous grimace, and turned the Taser on him again. This time the shock sent him to the floor, but at least the pain was over quickly.

"Gideon!" Maggie screamed.

But her cry was nearly obscured by the old woman's shouting. "Leave it alone. Leave it alone!" she screeched. "Why can't you just give up and go away? It's none of your business."

As Gideon struggled to his feet, the woman emphasized her words with another prod, sending his rigid body down flat again.

"No!" Maggie shouted, and Gideon was vaguely aware of her movement above him as he struggled to pull himself up again. Her hand swept past his eyes as she reached for the Taser as though to take it away from Lorna.

Gideon wanted to shout, to warn her, but her body went stiff and she dropped to one knee from what appeared to be a glancing stun.

"Keep out of it," Lorna screeched. "Keep out of my things! Keep out of my business!"

Blurring pain clouded his eyes as he attempted to lift his head. He had to get the Taser away from Lorna and get Lorna away from Maggie. And he had to get Maggie away from the wide-open window. In the course of their struggling, the two women had moved dangerously close to the open space where nothing stood between them and a three-story drop onto the brick patio below.

"Move away from the window," he groaned, his lips and his vocal cords still in rebellion from the series of shocks they'd received. The words came out inaudibly, even to his ears. As he attempted once again to pull himself to his feet, he saw Lorna's left hand go to her pocket.

"Watch her," he gasped, the words clearer this time. "Left hand."

Maggie glanced down, and he saw realization register on her face as her eyes focused on the woman's other hand. What did the woman have in her pocket? A gun?

Unable to stand the thought of Lorna using a deadly weapon on Maggie, Gideon fought past the immobilizing pain and struggled forward. As he neared the women, Lorna spun around, pressing the Taser to him once again.

"Stay down!" Lorna shouted.

"No!" Maggie screamed.

As the rigid shock released its hold on his body, Gideon saw Maggie take a swipe at Lorna's left hand. Whatever she'd been holding flew free, and he heard it hit the floor with a clatter and skitter under a nearby dresser.

"You!" Lorna turned her attention back to Maggie.

"You're just like your father. You can die, too!" The larger woman rushed at Maggie, pushing her toward the open window.

Gideon couldn't allow Lorna to push Maggie to the window. A fall from that height could kill her. Forcing his body to move in spite of his trembling muscles, Gideon lunged at them both, wrapping his numb arms around Maggie and falling sideways with her, his aching body still awkward and uncooperative.

As he spun around, his only goal to push Maggie as far from the window as possible, an aftershock pulsed through his leg muscles, sending his feet kicking outward in a herky-jerky motion. The numb nerve endings of his feet sent a message of pain to his brain as the soles of his feet made contact with Lorna's body.

A strangled scream echoed for a moment behind him, then faded as the woman fell from sight through the open window.

Gideon panted and he held Maggie tight in his arms as the reality of what had happened began to catch up with him.

He felt Maggie's hands sweep over his face. "Are you okay?" she asked, pulling her face into his line of sight. Her glasses were missing, probably knocked aside in the course of their struggles. "Gideon." Her hands caressed his brow, his cheeks. "Can you talk to me?"

"Where's your phone?" he asked as soon as he could make his lips work. "We need to call the sheriff."

"It's back over there," Maggie said in a whisper. "I can't reach it." She paused a moment. "You'll have to let go of me."

Gideon sighed. He didn't want to let go of her. He didn't want to ever let go of her. But she was right. There was far more at stake than his simple need to hold the woman he loved. Even though he didn't want to do anything more than wrap his arms around her and keep her close, they needed to call the sheriff. And Bernie Gills. Somebody would have to pick the lock on the box they'd found.

Loosening the hold he had on her, Gideon rolled onto his back, and Maggie crawled past him and reached for her phone. While she relayed their needs to the dispatcher, Gideon attempted to make his muscles carry him back to her side. They didn't want to obey. As soon as he got close to where she sat on the floor, he let his head fall onto her lap with a flump.

As Maggie's fingers caressed the side of his face, Gideon collected his thoughts and recalled the moment when Maggie had knocked something free from Lorna's left hand. What had it been?

Finding his flashlight where he'd dropped it earlier, Gideon crawled over to the dresser near the window and pointed his flashlight underneath. The beam glittered off of something shiny. It was far too small to be a gun. Cautiously, Gideon reached for the object and pulled it out from under the dresser.

"What did you find?" Maggie asked as she crouched down beside him.

"A key." Gideon held the brass object for her to see. He glanced to the locked box and then back to Maggie. The scrolling design again.

"The sheriff and an ambulance are on their way," Maggie updated him. "Should we wait?"

"We can wait to open the box," Gideon agreed, using the dresser to pull himself up into a standing position.

Maggie stepped closer, and he felt the supportive pull of her arms as she tried to help him up. "Are you sure you're okay?"

Allowing himself to lean on her slightly, Gideon pulled her into his embrace. "I think I'll be okay."

Though she didn't want to let go of Gideon, Maggie was relieved when the sheriff arrived a few moments later, and even more relieved when the paramedics pulled Lorna, unconscious but still breathing, from the roll-away Dumpster.

"All those trash bags cushioned her fall and probably saved her life," one of the medics concluded after Lorna had been loaded into the back of the ambulance.

"I'm glad," Maggie said softly. When Gideon looked at her questioningly, she explained, "I know Lorna is probably the person who pushed my father to his death, but that doesn't mean I wanted her to die. Besides, there are still so many things I don't understand. She's the only person who can answer our questions."

"We have a lot of questions, too," Sheriff Walker reminded them.

"But first—" Deputy Bernie Gills extended a hand to Gideon "—I owe you an apology. Lorna stole my Taser, didn't she?"

"It appears so," Gideon agreed simply, taking his former coworker's hand and shaking it. From where she stood a couple of feet from him, Maggie could feel Gideon's relief at Bernie's apology.

"I'm sorry I jumped to conclusions," Bernie stated simply. "With all the other charges against you—" The officer looked sheepish.

Gideon dismissed the older man's embarrassment. "I was the logical suspect," he offered. "Who would have ever thought…?" His voice trailed off as he looked back up at the attic window. "That reminds me. We still have a box to open."

As Kim and Bernie followed them into the house with curious faces, Maggie and Gideon led the officers back up to the attic.

"Lorna had this key in her pocket," Gideon explained, showing them the brass key. "I suspect it may open this box or the casket we found, or both. Either way, this may be the object Lorna was looking for when she searched Glen Arnold's pockets after he died. Only Lorna can tell us for sure." His eyes met Maggie's for a moment.

She felt the weight of his words and saw the apology in his eyes. But he had nothing to be sorry for. He'd helped to capture her father's killer. "Can we see if it opens the box?" she asked quietly.

Gideon bent down beside the wooden box. "Shall I?" he asked.

With the officers' permission, Gideon turned the key and opened the lid.

A glittering array of jewels and flashing gold met their eyes. "It's like a treasure chest," Maggie said softly, stunned by the opulent riches that had been hidden under the eaves, unknown to her.

"Where did all of this come from?" Bernie asked, his eyes wide.

"I wonder if Lorna hid it here," Maggie mused aloud. "But where did she get it all? Do you think those jewels are real?"

Gideon reached toward a larger gold object. "May I?" he asked the sheriff before touching it.

Kim nodded. "Go ahead. What is it?"

"A pocket watch." Gideon held up the gold obelisk by its long chain. "I wonder if this is the one Dan Creel was looking for?"

"I can ask him," Kim offered. "He should be arriving in Holyoake later today to ID the body we found."

"Which we thought was his mother's," Maggie said, the disparity plaguing her. "But if that wasn't Lorna Creel in the casket, then who was it? Her face certainly resembled Lorna's."

"I've been thinking about that," Bernie spoke up. "Lorna wasn't from around here. She didn't have any family in the area, but I seem to recall when her mother died they had the funeral here."

"In Holyoake?" Kim asked.

"In this house," Bernie clarified. "Remember, this used to be a funeral home. That was years ago, but then, if that body has been down there a while…" His voice faded.

Maggie understood what the deputy was getting at. "If the body was Lorna's mother, that would explain why she looked so much like her."

"And why none of us recognized her," Gideon added. "None of us had ever met her mother."

"But Dan Creel should be able to recognize his own grandmother, don't you think?" Kim concluded, taking a step back and looking at her watch. "Speaking of which, he said he'd be at the sheriff's office at eight this morning, as soon as his plane got in. Since I need to meet with him anyway, I'm going to run over there now. We have a lot of questions for him. Then I'll see if he wants to come with me when I go to question Lorna."

"Sure thing," Bernie agreed. "I'll meet you at the hospital when I'm done talking to these two."

By the time Bernie Gills left the House on Shady Oak Lane, Maggie was exhausted. She felt as though she still had more questions than answers. To make matters worse, Gideon had left as soon as the deputy was gone, leaving Maggie feeling all alone in the big empty house. Though she'd lived there for weeks and weeks, she'd never felt so lost in the place. So much had happened that she needed to sort out.

In spite of all the puzzles that still surrounded the case, Maggie couldn't tear her thoughts away from Gideon. She had been so frightened when Lorna had used the Taser on him, and not just because of her fears that he might be hurt. Though she'd tried to push back her growing feelings for Gideon during the time they'd been working together on the house, she couldn't push away reality.

She loved Gideon.

Seeing him writhing in pain had torn at her heart more than all the suffering of the sick children she'd cared for in the pediatric ward. She'd never thought anything could hurt more than seeing an innocent child suffering from an illness or injury. But seeing Gideon tortured by Lorna had been more painful still.

Maggie paced the house several times over the rest of the day. She made herself a cup of coffee. She made herself a bowl of soup. Over and over again, she found herself frozen in a daze, staring at some random part of the house they'd been working on.

She'd stood for nearly half an hour looking at the woodwork they'd refinished in the parlor. The rich warm colors of the wood had been hiding under suffocating layers of paint for decades, but their hard work and elbow grease had revealed its true beauty.

Everywhere throughout the house she saw new glimpses of what the fully finished house would eventually look like. As Gideon had predicted, the place would eventually look spectacular. She wished she could stick around to see it done. She'd even begun to warm up to the idea of knocking out the back wall and expanding the kitchen after all, especially after the fire had damaged so much of the existing exterior. If they had to redo it anyway, they might as well redo it for maximum effect.

After nearly losing the house to fire the day before, and then being faced with the possibility that the house should have rightfully gone to Lorna's children, Maggie had realized how much she cared for the place and longed to see it made right. She'd even caught herself imagining what it would be like to live there.

But as her loneliness closed in on her in Gideon's absence, she realized she couldn't stand to stay in the place without him. Every piece of the house they'd worked on together held memories of him. Living there without him would be torture.

Her agitated heart churned fitfully within her all day, and she was about to give up and try to get some sleep that evening when headlights flashed against the house and moments later she heard the familiar footfall of Gideon's steps on the front porch.

When Gideon opened the door Maggie saw that he looked tired. More than tired—exhausted. Red lines rimmed his dark eyes.

She was at his side in a moment. "Are you okay? Can I get you something?"

To her surprise, Gideon closed the door behind him, then reached for her and pulled her into his arms, holding her tight for a long moment. "This is what I need," he said as he held her close.

Blinking back the tears that threatened to fall at the feel of his arms around her, Maggie relished the comforting feeling of being so close to him. "Where have you been?"

"I went to see my brother."

"Bruce?" Maggie pulled away just enough so she could see into Gideon's face.

Gideon nodded. "I should have gone sooner. I was just too angry with him. But I realized that I had to talk to him about what happened twenty years ago, about how his lies hurt you and hurt me."

Maggie's eyes widened. "How did it go?"

A slow smile eased across Gideon's weary face. "Better than I'd hoped. I think Bruce's conscience is finally starting to catch up to him. He admitted to me that Kayla's illness all those years ago was caused by the meth he was making in the house. He tried to clean up his act after that, but then he needed money for her medical bills and didn't see any other way out." Gideon shook his head regretfully.

"I told him I'd be praying for him."

"How did he respond to that?" Maggie asked.

"I think he was genuinely glad to hear it—and glad for my visit once he figured out I wasn't there to yell at him. I'm glad I went." The words were barely spoken when his phone began to ring.

"It's Sheriff Walker," Gideon said, looking at the caller ID.

"Answer it," Maggie urged him, and followed him to the threadbare Victorian sofa in the parlor where they sat side by side with their heads together and the volume turned up on the phone so both of them could hear.

"We finally have some answers," Kim Walker informed them in a satisfied voice. "The body we found in your basement was that of Lorna Creel's mother. She died eighteen years ago when Lorna was working at the funeral home. It seems Lorna had been secretly stealing jewelry from the bodies over the years—that's where the stash in the attic came from."

"How could she get away with that?" Maggie asked, almost in spite of herself.

"I wondered the same thing," Kim explained. "Fortunately, Len Turner, the mortician she worked for, was available to speak with us. He's quite old but still very sharp and explained that Lorna was in charge of the final preparations before they closed the casket the last time, as the mourners headed out to their cars to go to the cemetery. She was often alone with the body for several minutes. Sadly, Len had complete trust in her, even though he shouldn't have."

"But how did her mother's body end up in the basement?" Gideon questioned.

Kim sighed. "As near as we can piece together from what Lorna was willing to tell us, her mother had requested to be buried in the family jewelry. Lorna's siblings insisted on following her mother's request, but Lorna couldn't stand the idea and tried to remove the jewelry just as she had stolen from other people over the years. When she couldn't get it off, she pulled her mother's body from the casket, hid it in a closet and packed dead weight in the coffin."

Kim's voice took on a slightly amused tone. "We had her mother's coffin exhumed this afternoon. It was full of old magazines and a ten-pound sack of sugar. Lorna later placed the body in a different coffin and hid it in the basement wall."

"So why didn't she just take the box of jewelry with her when she moved out? Lorna looked like she could still carry it, even though it was pretty heavy."

"That's where the story gets a little bit more complicated," Kim explained. "We suspect Lorna was suffering from kleptomania, among other mental disorders. When the house was foreclosed on, Lorna's daughter, Linda, took her to live with her. Apparently Lorna feared that if she took the box with her, Linda would learn of its contents.

Linda knew her mother had issues with mental illness, but she thought her home was the safest place for her. Unfortunately, it seems there were times when Lorna snuck out of the house. That's when she got into trouble."

"That's why things kept disappearing in spurts, and then we'd go weeks without an incident," Maggie concluded aloud.

"Exactly," Kim concurred. "Whenever her mother disappeared, Linda would watch her more carefully for a while. But as soon as she let her guard down Lorna would sneak away. We've matched her fingerprints to the gas can we found the day of the fire. They also match the fingerprints found on the note left in your door, and on your father's wallet the day he died."

Even though she'd suspected as much, the news still caused Maggie's throat to tighten. "She killed him and searched his pockets?"

"Yes. She'd left the brass key in the lock of the coffin. When your father found it, Lorna feared he'd also find her treasure chest in the attic. She tried to find the key, but obviously your father had hidden it in his glove box. You found it there, and kept it on your key ring until Lorna stole it back again. We have the rest of your keys to give back to you now, too."

The last bit of Kim's words were obscured by Gideon's phone beeping.

"I'm sorry, Sheriff. I have another call coming in," he apologized.

"That's fine. I've told you everything we've learned. You have a good evening."

"You, too. Thank you." Gideon switched over to answer the incoming call.

Since he still had the volume turned up high, and since Maggie was still sitting so close to him on the sofa, she could clearly hear the words of the man on the other end, who introduced himself as being from the County Board of Supervisors.

Maggie felt her hopes rise as the man spoke.

"The DEA has informed us that they received a phone call from your brother's lawyer this afternoon. Bruce has decided to change his plea to guilty on all charges. Based on his confession, which corresponds to the evidence they've gathered, it appears we no longer have any charges to hold against you. We'll have to have another hearing to make it official, but I knew you'd want to know as soon as possible."

"So I'll be able to return to my job as sheriff?" Gideon clarified.

"As soon as it's made official, yes, all charges will be dropped and you can return to your former position."

While Gideon exhaled a sigh of relief, Maggie felt as if her emotions had been thrown into turmoil. She was infinitely glad for him that he'd been cleared of the charges. Part of her felt like leaping into the air and shouting for joy. But another part of her felt crushed by the implications of his exoneration.

If Gideon went back to his job as sheriff, he wouldn't have time to continue working with her on the house. What would become of the place then?

"Did you hear?" Gideon asked, turning to face her after he'd thanked the man again and closed the call.

"Yes." She didn't have to work too hard to put on a smile for his benefit. She really did feel happy for him. "That's wonderful news. I'm so glad for you."

"Are you sure?" His intent dark eyes probed her face. "You don't look so glad."

With a frown of embarrassment, Maggie admitted, "I guess I was hoping for more time to work on the house with you. But I understand..." Her voice trailed off as Gideon grabbed her hands and held them to his lips.

"I'm relieved to hear you feel that way about the house," Gideon murmured as his lips brushed her fingertips.

Maggie found it difficult to think. It had been a long day already, and the man she loved was kissing her fingers. "Why?" she asked softly once she'd mustered enough presence of mind to utter that syllable.

"I never got to finish telling you the other part of my good news," he reminded her, opening the Bible he'd carried down from upstairs. "Your father gave me this Bible when I graduated from college," he explained. "He underlined a verse for me, but I never really understood it until now."

"'Unless the Lord builds the house, its builders labor in vain,'" Gideon read. "I thought this verse was about building a house, like the houses your father and I worked on together all those summers that I worked for him. But as I was reading elsewhere in the Bible, I realized *house* often stands for a person's *household,* for a person's *family.* Look at verse three."

Gideon read, "'Sons are a heritage from the Lord, children are a reward from Him.'" His eyes glittered as he looked Maggie full in the face and continued explaining. "The Lord didn't build the household I grew up in. We were raised without faith, and look where it got us? My brother will probably spend the rest of his life in prison."

Gideon set the book beside them on the sofa and scooped up Maggie's hands into his again. "I don't want to lead an empty life. I want to build a household with the Lord, and with you. I keep thinking about this house and imagining what it would be like to live here, to work beside you in the kitchen, to fill all those bedrooms upstairs with kids. I could sell my house and we could use the money to name a room in the hospital after your father."

"Oh, Gideon," Maggie gasped, her heart overflowing at the beautiful picture he painted with his words. Was it possible that they could marry and live in the house together? It would be like a dream come true. It was more than she'd even hoped for. "You really want to do that?"

"I do." He grinned at her. "Do you?"

"I do." She smiled back. "More than anything."

"Then you'll marry me?" Gideon asked.

"Yes!"

"Good." Gideon smiled as he leaned toward her and kissed her on the lips.

* * * * *

Dear Reader,

On my second visit to the gutted house that is now my home, I discovered the cellar door had been pushed in as though someone had broken into the house. It was a creepy feeling to stand there in that dank basement and realize the security of the structure had been compromised. In my case, the crime was fairly innocent. But in Maggie's case there was obviously much more going on.

I have been so blessed to write this book! Though it was inspired by my own experiences fixing up an abused old house, Gideon and Maggie's adventures were entirely their own. I'm so glad I didn't encounter any of the troubles they met up with…except for a few bats. And that cellar break-in. But there are no dead bodies in my house. Honest!

I hope you've enjoyed this visit to Holyoake, Iowa. If you missed the first of the Holyoake Heroes books, I invite you to look for *Out on a Limb,* where we met Gideon Bromley for the very first time. And please continue to look for more of my stories. You can find current information on all my forthcoming titles on my website at *www.rachellemccalla.com.*

In Christ,

Rachelle McCalla

QUESTIONS FOR DISCUSSION

1. Maggie had prayed the handyman she'd called would be willing to work on her house. But when she recognized Gideon Bromley, a man who she felt ashamed to face, she had second thoughts about asking him to take on the job. Has God ever answered your prayers in an unexpected way? How did you respond?

2. When Gideon first learned that Glen Arnold's death was ruled an accident, he was reluctant to share his suspicions with Maggie. Have you ever hidden something from another person because you didn't want them to be hurt? Was that the right choice in your situation? Why or why not?

3. Though Deputy Bernie Gills makes no apology for his attacks on Gideon, the former sheriff doesn't argue with his onetime coworker. Have you ever been blamed for something you didn't do? How did you respond? Why does Gideon respond the way he does? Do you believe his response was appropriate?

4. Maggie insists on staying in the spooky old house where her father was killed because she feels she has no other choice, and she trusts in God to protect her. Do you believe her decision was wise? Have you ever chosen to do something others may have seen as foolhardy? How did that turn out for you? Would you make the same decision again?

5. Gideon blames himself for Glen Arnold's death because he didn't arrive in time to stop the murderer

from killing him. Do you believe Gideon's guilt is warranted? What might you have done in his shoes?

6. Even though Gideon is suspended from his job as sheriff, he takes comfort in being able to help Maggie. Have you ever had a cherished job taken away from you? Were you able to find new, fulfilling roles? How does Gideon's story help you to understand how others feel when they retire or step down from long-held positions?

7. Maggie and Gideon feel a connection to each other through their prior relationships with Maggie's deceased father. How has a second-degree connection helped you to bond with someone else more quickly? Was that good for your relationship, or were there negative consequences? What are the risks and benefits of trusting someone simply because another person you know has trusted them?

8. Maggie and Gideon have different views about Rex Dunham's questionable ethics and whether that should influence Maggie's decision to sell to the man. Do you believe Maggie made the right choice? What might you have done differently?

9. Because Gideon was so focused on investigating Glen Arnold's murder, he didn't respond immediately to tips he received about a possible drug lab, and his actions made him look as if he'd been covering for his brother. But according to police procedure, a homicide investigation should take precedence even over a narcotics investigation. So Gideon did the

right thing, but for a long time it looked as though he would be punished for his decision. Have you ever been punished for making a choice you felt was right? What happened?

10. Gideon trusted his brother because he looked up to him. Similarly, Kayla had been exposed to possible clues about her father's drug activities while she was growing up, but she still didn't know what he was up to. Have you ever been surprised by the secrets people are able to hide from their loved ones? Have you ever failed to see through someone's actions because you respected them? Do you believe people can be blinded by trust? Is this a good thing or a bad thing—or does it just depend on the situation?

11. Gideon compares Maggie and Kayla to sheep, his brother Bruce to a wolf and himself to a sheepdog. What do you think of his analogy? Which role fits you most closely: sheep, wolf or sheepdog? Why?

12. Both Maggie and Gideon feel condemned by the lies Bruce told about them over the years, but they trust in God's promise that those who trust in Him will never be condemned. Do you think their faith is realistic? Why or why not?

13. Maggie and Gideon are both quiet people who have learned to read each other without necessarily talking things through. How is this good for their relationship? What are some of the drawbacks? Have you ever assumed you knew how someone else felt, only to later be surprised by their true feelings?

14. Gideon is reluctant to let on to Maggie about his growing feelings for her because he's afraid he'll end up in prison. Do you think he made the right choice? What are the costs of his decision?

15. Maggie's father gave Gideon a Bible years before, but it's not until after Glen is dead that Gideon begins to read the Bible and understand about God's love for him. Have you ever planted seeds of faith that you may never see grow? Does Maggie and Gideon's story encourage you to continue sharing your faith with others?

Love Inspired ®
SUSPENSE

TITLES AVAILABLE NEXT MONTH

Available February 8, 2011

REQUEST YOUR FREE BOOKS!

2 FREE RIVETING INSPIRATIONAL NOVELS
PLUS 2 FREE MYSTERY GIFTS

Love Inspired®
SUSPENSE

YES! Please send me 2 FREE Love Inspired® Suspense novels and my 2 FREE mystery gifts (gifts are worth about $10). After receiving them, if I don't wish to receive any more books, I can return the shipping statement marked "cancel". If I don't cancel, I will receive 4 brand-new novels every month and be billed just $4.24 per book in the U.S. or $4.74 per book in Canada. That's a saving of 20% off the cover price. It's quite a bargain! Shipping and handling is just 50¢ per book.* I understand that accepting the 2 free books and gifts places me under no obligation to buy anything. I can always return a shipment and cancel at any time. Even if I never buy another book, the two free books and gifts are mine to keep forever.

123/323 IDN E7QZ

Name _____ (PLEASE PRINT)

Address _____ Apt. #

City _____ State/Prov. _____ Zip/Postal Code

Signature (if under 18, a parent or guardian must sign)

Mail to **Steeple Hill Reader Service:**
IN U.S.A.: P.O. Box 1867, Buffalo, NY 14240-1867
IN CANADA: P.O. Box 609, Fort Erie, Ontario L2A 5X3

Not valid for current subscribers to Love Inspired Suspense books.

Want to try two free books from another series?
Call 1-800-873-8635 or visit www.morefreebooks.com.

* Terms and prices subject to change without notice. Prices do not include applicable taxes. Sales tax applicable in N.Y. Canadian residents will be charged applicable provincial taxes and GST. Offer not valid in Quebec. This offer is limited to one order per household. All orders subject to approval. Credit or debit balances in a customer's account(s) may be offset by any other outstanding balance owed by or to the customer. Please allow 4 to 6 weeks for delivery. Offer available while quantities last.

Your Privacy: Steeple Hill Books is committed to protecting your privacy. Our Privacy Policy is available online at www.SteepleHill.com or upon request from the Reader Service. From time to time we make our lists of customers available to reputable third parties who may have a product or service of interest to you. If you would prefer we not share your name and address, please check here. ☐

Help us get it right—We strive for accurate, respectful and relevant communications. To clarify or modify your communication preferences, visit us at www.ReaderService.com/consumerschoice.

LISUS10R

Enjoy a sneak peek at Valerie Hansen's adventurous historical-romance novel RESCUING THE HEIRESS, available February, only from Love Inspired Historical

"I think your profession is most honorable."

One more quick glance showed him that Tess was smiling, and it was all he could do to keep from breaking into a face-splitting grin at her praise. There was something impish yet charming about the banker's daughter. Always had been, if he were totally honest with himself.

Someday, Michael vowed silently, he would find a suitable woman with a spirit like Tess's and give her a proper courting. He had no chance with Tess herself, of course. That went without saying. Still, she couldn't be the only appealing lass in San Francisco. Besides, most men waited to wed until they could properly look after a wife and family.

If he'd been a rich man's son instead of the offspring of a lowly sailor, however, perhaps he'd have shown a personal interest in Miss Clark or one of her socialite friends already.

Would he really have? he asked himself. He doubted it. There was a part of Michael that was repelled by the affectations of the wealthy, by the way they lorded it over the likes of him and his widowed mother. He knew Tess couldn't help that she'd been born into a life of luxury, yet he still found her background off-putting.

Which is just as well, he reminded himself. It was bad enough that they were likely to be seen out and about on this particular evening. If the maid Annie Dugan hadn't been along as a chaperone, he knew their time together could, if misinterpreted, lead to his ruination. His career with the fire department depended upon a sterling reputation as well as a

Spartan lifestyle and strong work ethic.

Michael had labored too long and hard to let anything spoil his pending promotion to captain. He set his jaw and grasped the reins of the carriage more tightly. Not even the prettiest, smartest, most persuasive girl in San Francisco was going to get away with doing that.

He sighed, realizing that Miss Tess Clark fit that description to a T.

You won't be able to put down the rest of
Tess and Michael's romantic love story,
available in February 2011,
only from Love Inspired Historical.

Love Inspired.
HISTORICAL
INSPIRATIONAL HISTORICAL ROMANCE

Dr. Ben Drake has always held a special place in his heart for strays. The ultimate test of his compassion comes when the fragile beauty at his door is revealed to be his brother's widow. Callie could expose the Drakes' darkest family secrets but just one look at her and Ben knows he can't turn her away—not when he can lead her to true love and God's forgiving grace.

Rocky Mountain Redemption
by
PAMELA NISSEN

*Available February
wherever books are sold.*

www.SteepleHill.com

Steeple
Hill®

LiH82857